Praise for
Dinner with a Perfect Stranger

"Here's a wonderful feast for the mind and soul! Pull up a chair and eavesdrop on this provocative conversation. If you're like me, you'll hear questions that match your own—and answers that can change your life."

—LEE STROBEL, author of *The Case for Christ, The Case for Faith,* and *The Case for a Creator*

"There's just one thing people need in order to live a happy, abundant life: to be convinced that God loves them. Want to be convinced? Read *Dinner with a Perfect Stranger.* The author deftly anticipates and answers every question. I predict this little book will become a classic—one of a handful of modern books (like *Mere Christianity*) that people read to kindle or rekindle faith. All of the "business" surrounding the dinner is done so well it reminds me of *Babette's Feast*—simple, earthy details that profoundly convey spiritual reality. *Dinner with a Perfect Stranger* is truly a wonderful book that makes me feel I've just heard the gospel for the very first time."

—MIKE MASON, author of *The Mystery of Marriage, Champagne for the Soul,* and *Practicing the Presence of People*

"The choice is yours: Enjoy a delicious meal of, say, veal fantarella with grilled vegetables. Or spend a quiet hour reading David Gregory's book. You may find an altogether different sort of hunger has been sated by the final page. Brilliant in its simplicity, fearless in its presentation of the truth, *Dinner with a Perfect Stranger* is one invitation you'll want to RSVP."

—LIZ CURTIS HIGGS, author of *Thorn in My Heart, Fair Is the Rose,* and *Whence Came a Prince*

DINNER
WITH A PERFECT
STRANGER

Dinner with a Perfect Stranger

WITH A **PERFECT**

STRANGER

An Invitation Worth Considering

DAVID GREGORY

WATERBROOK
PRESS

DINNER WITH A PERFECT STRANGER

The Scripture quotation is based on the New International Version and the New American Standard Bible. Holy Bible, New International Version®. NIV®. Copyright © 1973, 1978, 1984 by International Bible Society. Used by permission of Zondervan Publishing House. All rights reserved. New American Standard Bible® (nasb). © Copyright The Lockman Foundation 1960, 1962, 1963, 1968, 1971, 1972, 1973, 1975, 1977, 1995. Used by permission. (www.Lockman.org).

The events and characters (except for Jesus Christ) in this book are fictional, and any resemblance to actual events or persons is coincidental.

Trade Paperback ISBN 978-0-307-73009-1
eBook ISBN 978-0-307-44630-5

Published in the United States by WaterBrook, an imprint of the Crown Publishing Group, a division of Penguin Random House LLC, New York.

WATERBROOK® and its deer colophon are registered trademarks of Penguin Random House LLC.

The Library of Congress cataloged the hardcover edition as follows:
Gregory, David, 1959-
    Dinner with a perfect stranger : an invitation worth considering / David Gregory.—
1st WaterBrook ed.
    p. cm.
    ISBN 1-57856-905-2
    1. Jesus Christ—Fiction. 2. Dinners and dining—Fiction.
3. Restaurants—Fiction. 4. Imaginary conversations. I. Title.
    PS3607.R4884D56 2005
    813'.6—dc22

                                            2005001761

Printed in the United States of America

15

SPECIAL SALES
Most WaterBrook books are available in special quantity discounts when purchased in bulk by corporations, organizations and special interest groups. Custom imprinting or excerpting can also be done to fit special needs. For information, please e-mail specialmarketscms@penguinrandomhouse.com or call 1-800-603-7051.

To Rick and Denise,
who made this book possible

Acknowledgments

My thanks to Howard Hendricks, Reg Grant, Scott Horrell, and Mike Moore for providing inspiration to venture outside my box, and to Sandi Glahn for coaching me.

To those who provided feedback on the manuscript, the readers say thanks (I hope). So do I. My special thanks to Rex Purkerson and Mallory Dubuclet for your unique contributions and to Bruce Nygren for seeing this project through to completion.

In the dog days of manuscript editing, every writer needs a downpour of encouragement to get through the final stages. Dad, you provided that encouragement.

Finally, to my wife, Ava, thank you for all your help with ideas and editing, for your patience, and for your contagious excitement about this book. You are a wonderful partner and a keen editor to boot.

The Invitation

I SHOULD HAVE known better than to respond. My personal planner was full enough without accepting anonymous invitations to dine with religious leaders. Especially dead ones.

Amid a stack of credit card applications and professional society junk, the invitation arrived at my work address:

Nick Cominsky
Director of Strategic Planning
Pruitt Environmental Testing
1825 Landover Street
Cincinnati, Ohio 45230

It came typeset on beige Crane paper with matching envelope. No return address. No RSVP.

You are invited

to a dinner

with

Jesus of Nazareth

❧

Milano's Restaurant

Tuesday, March 24 • Eight o'clock

At first I thought the church down the street was having another one of their "outreaches." We had been outreached on more than one occasion. Their mailbox flier awaited us the minute my wife, Mattie, and I moved here from Chicago three years ago. An endless stream of what some church worker considered promotional material followed. I actually started looking forward to them, just for the amusement the sermon titles provided:

The Ten Commandments, Not the Ten Suggestions
If God Seems Far Away, Guess Who Moved?
Spiritual Aerobics for the Marathon to Heaven

Did they mean to attract anyone with those or just make the neighborhood disdain them?

Then came the events: the church bowling-league invitation, the spaghetti cookoff, the marriage-retreat weekend, the golf-scramble invitation. In a moment of insanity I actually broke down and went to the golf scramble. Utter agony is the only way to describe it. Parking at the course behind a guy with a "My Boss Is a Jewish Carpenter" bumper sticker set the tone. As it turned out, I was assigned to his foursome. He had this perpetual smile, as though someone had hit him with a brick and the plastic surgeon had patched him up on an off day. As for the other two, one guy shot a nice front nine but fell apart on the back nine and started swearing every time he hit a shot. I learned he headed the deacon board. The other guy never said a word except to track our score. He must have chaired the welcoming committee. That was the last church invitation I accepted.

So if that church had concocted it, there was no way I was going to this bogus dinner. But the more I thought about it, the more I concluded that someone else had sent the invitation. For one thing, how would the church have my work address? They were persistent but not particularly resourceful. For another, this just wasn't that church's style. The spaghetti cookoff was more their bag than Milano's, an upscale Italian restaurant. Besides, they would never send an anonymous invitation. If there was one thing they wanted you to know, it was that *their* church was sponsoring an event.

That left me in a quandary. Who would send me such an odd invitation? I called the restaurant, but they denied knowing anything. Of course, the staff could have agreed to play dumb about it, so that told me little. Cincinnati had lots of other churches, but I'd successfully avoided all contact with them. Our friends Dave and Paula went to the Unity Church, but they wouldn't invite me to something like this without Mattie.

One logical set of culprits remained: the guys at work. Les and Bill in particular were always putting together something crazy, like my bachelor party at a local mortuary and my guy baby shower (thankfully, they left Mattie off the invitation list; I'd never seen such a raunchy celebration for the birth of a baby). I admit, this invitation seemed a bit strange even for those guys. And they should have known better than to send me the invitation at work. It was too obvious. Otherwise they had done a pretty good job: classy envelope and printing, bizarre event, nice restaurant.

I decided to play it cool with them, never mentioning the invite. And for three full weeks they kept cool too, letting slip not so much as a sly grin. As the twenty-fourth approached, my anticipation grew, wondering what their fertile imaginations had conceived this time.

Only one thing stood between the dinner and me: Mattie. Three seventy-hour workweeks had already placed me deep in the doghouse with my other half, who chafed at even my usual sixty-hour pace. I couldn't think how to justify a night out with the guys, leaving her home again with Sara, our daughter.

Granted, it's hard looking after a twenty-month-old by yourself all day and then all evening, too. Not to mention that Mattie ran a home graphics business on the side. If we had stayed in Chicago, either of our mothers could have helped her out with Sara. Well, hers anyway. My mother would have squealed at the chance to keep the baby, but

staying at her house too often would probably have made
Sara...like me. Hopefully, the three hundred miles between
Cincinnati and Chicago sufficiently insulated my daughter
from that fate.

Mattie knew when she moved to Cincinnati with me
and we married that I'd be working long hours. You can't
have a job like mine and clock out at five. I can just imagine
waving my hand at Jim, my boss, as I pass by his office on
my way out. "Sorry, man, got to go again. Mattie needs
me home at five thirty to dice Sara's vegetables." A few five
o'clock departures and Jim would insist I stay home as a full-
time nanny.

I can see my résumé now:

EDUCATION

BS, Chemistry, Northern Illinois University, 1996

MBA, Northwestern University, 2001

WORK HISTORY

Research Chemist, Abbott Laboratories, 1996–2000

Corporate Planning Analyst, Abbott Laboratories,
2000–2002

Director of Strategic Planning, Pruitt Environmental
Testing, 2002–2005

Nanny, 2005 to present

Keeping my current job seemed preferable, despite the dangers it presented. Truth was, between the pile on my desk at work and Mattie's perpetual displeasure at home, getting away from both for an evening appealed to me. I just wondered whether Milano's knew what it was getting into with Les's and Bill's antics.

The restaurant's problems were far from my mind, though, as I approached its parking lot. Mattie shouting into the cell phone, "Nick, I might as well be a single parent for all you—" were the last words I heard on the way over before static saved me. That was enough. I never had figured out how to rationalize my plans for the evening. In retrospect, I should have given her more than twenty minutes' notice.

Blasting some R.E.M. while speeding down Anderson Ferry didn't completely drown my guilt, but it gave it a good dunking. I pulled the Explorer into the parking lot, cut the engine, and reached once more for the invitation, hoping it would give me one last hint about what to expect for the evening. It didn't. Suddenly nothing about this dinner seemed worth the cold shoulder I would get from Mattie later on.

I was here, though. And if the whole event was a washout, I could save face with Mattie by leaving early. Showing up at home sooner than expected at least once a month seemed to buy me a little grace. After the last three weeks, I needed some—badly.

Contingency plan in hand, I crossed the parking lot, breached the threshold, and glanced around the twenty or so tables. No guys with long hair in flowing robes. No guys from work, either.

2

The Seating

"DINNER FOR ONE, sir?"

The maître d's appearance from behind the wine bar dashed my option of bolting before anyone noticed me.

"Sir? Dinner for one?"

"No, I'm…I'm supposed to meet someone. I'm Nick Cominsky…"

"Ah, Mr. Cominsky. Right this way."

He grabbed a menu and led me past the wood lattice that bordered the single dining room. The place hadn't changed since I had brought Mattie for Valentine's two years back. Two staggered tablecloths, one white and one red, covered each of the tables. Large mirrors created the image of a side dining area. The windows on two sides of the room overlooked the Ohio River. I could see lights from the Kentucky side reflecting on the water. The current provided nice background noise, like those ocean CDs you can buy to help you sleep. Unfortunately, some lame Andrea Bocelli song that Mattie loved virtually drowned out the river.

Tuesdays looked slow at Milano's. Guests occupied only four tables. I inhaled the smell of toasted bread as we passed an older party of six laughing at a front table. A couple in their early twenties held hands and made goo-goo eyes at each other in the far right corner, the guy oblivious to his shirt sleeve dangling in his ravioli. In the middle of the room, two weight-challenged women giggled as they plunged into a monstrous chocolate torte. And in the far corner on the left, a thirty-something man in a blue business suit sat by himself, perusing a menu.

The maître d' led me over to him. Rising from his chair, he stuck out his hand and firmly grasped mine.

"Nick Cominsky," he said. "Hi. Jesus."

In retrospect, a thousand comebacks were possible— "Jesus H. Christ! So good to finally meet you!"…"Are twelve of our party missing?"…"I didn't know they buried you in a suit."

The absurdity of the scene, though, stunned me into silence. What do you say to that? The man and I continued shaking hands a little too long, until I issued a weak "Uh-huh." He released my hand and sat back down.

My eyes caught the maître d's. He quickly averted his

glance and picked my napkin off my plate, cueing me to sit. He placed the napkin in my lap, handed me a menu and, with an "Enjoy your dinner," left me alone with...

"Thanks for meeting me," the man started. "This probably wasn't the most convenient time for you, middle of the week."

We stared at each other. Well, I stared. He resumed looking at his menu. He had an average build and was a little shorter than me, maybe five foot ten or so. His complexion toned olive, his hair dark and wavy, cut short and combed forward. His bushy eyebrows (*Mattie would make me trim those*, I thought) hung over deep eye sockets and brown eyes dark enough that you couldn't quite tell where the iris ended and the pupil began. His slender nose and thinnish lips matched a chin that receded slightly, as if knowing it couldn't compete with the brows above. He wasn't *GQ* cover material, but he definitely spent more time in the gym than I did. His suit wasn't Armani, but it wasn't Discount Warehouse, either.

He looked up and caught me scrutinizing him, but he didn't seem the least bit uncomfortable. Since my eyes provided few clues as to what this whole thing was about, I decided to give my ears a shot.

"Excuse me, but am I supposed to know you?"

"That's a good question," he smiled, to himself I guess. "I would say the answer is yes."

"I'm sorry, but I've never met you, as far as I can remember."

"That's true."

I looked around the room, waiting for the guys to jump out from behind the lattice or maybe from the men's room. But no one hid behind the lattice. As for the men's room… I turned my attention to the guy across the table.

"Come at me again. You are…"

"Jesus. My family called me Yeshua."

"Your family, from…"

"Nazareth."

"Of course."

"Well, I grew up there. I wasn't born there."

"No, of course not. That would have been in…"

"Bethlehem. But we didn't stay long before we left for Egypt."

That was about all I needed to hear. This guy was a nut. Without saying a word, I got up, retraced my steps past the lattice, took a right, and entered the bathroom. Mr. Ravioli was rinsing off his sleeve, but besides him, no one. Backing out, I momentarily considered cracking the door to the women's room, but I wasn't that desperate to find Les and Bill. I took a left and peeked through the circular window to the kitchen. Nothing. I paused, scanned the restaurant, and, deciding this warranted a more direct approach, returned to the table.

"Look," I said, sitting on the edge of my chair, "I've got better things to do tonight than have some mystery dinner with... Who are you really, and what's going on here?" My question had an unintended edge. After all, the guy hadn't done anything to me except meet for dinner.

"I know this isn't quite what you expected. But I think if you give this evening a try, you'll find it meaningful."

"Of course!" I retorted. "Who wouldn't find a dinner with Jesus meaningful? Last week I had dinner with Napoleon. Socrates the week before. But Jesus! Thank you so much for coming all the way from the Holy Land!" I realized my voice was carrying more than I wanted. The two women had turned our way.

He sat silently.

"Hey"—I rose again from my chair—"I need to get home to my wife and daughter. Thanks for the invitation." I stuck out my hand in a conciliatory gesture.

"Mattie went out to a movie with Jill," he said without flinching. "She got Rebecca to baby-sit Sara."

Okay. Finally a few pieces were starting to fall into place. He knew my wife. He knew Jill Conklin, the wife of my best friend, Chris. He knew our regular baby-sitter, Rebecca. He knew Mattie and Jill had gone to a movie. Once more I reclaimed my seat.

"Did Chris put you up to this?" I couldn't imagine how Chris could be involved; it was way too weird for him.

"No, he didn't."

I returned to my original suspects. "Are you a friend of Bill Grier and Les Kassler?"

He slid his menu aside and leaned forward. "I'll tell you what. If you stay for dinner, I promise to tell you at the end who set it up."

The last time Bill and Les had done something like this, I ended up wearing fake cement overshoes and getting tossed into a swimming pool on Halloween. A heated pool, fortunately. Now I was having dinner with some guy claiming to be Jesus.

The waiter interrupted my thoughts, addressing the man across the table. "Have you selected a wine, sir?"

"I think I'll let my friend decide," he responded, turning to me. "Would you care for some wine?"

"Who's paying?"

"I am."

"Okay," I replied, "sure."

I opened the wine list and scanned thirty or so offerings, none of which I recognized. I was tempted to order the most expensive one on the list, but instead I pointed to a midrange white. "We'll take the Kalike."

I handed the wine list to the waiter. He looked back at my host, who gave a slight nod.

"The Vermentino di Gallura–Kalike '98," the waiter confirmed to me. He departed, passing a busboy with a water pitcher. The busboy filled my glass first, then the other guy's, eliciting a "Thank you, Carlo."

We both picked up our water glasses and took a drink. I had to admit, this guy was good. Where did they find someone willing to play Jesus for an evening? And in such an unassuming way, as if he were just a normal guy. My co-workers had outdone themselves this time. But why? What was the point to all this? Les and Bill weren't particularly religious. Bill went to Mass on Christmas and Easter, when his wife dragged him there. As for Les, he worshiped only at Western Hills Country Club.

Glancing back over at the pre-honeymooners, the mirror caught my eye. Could the restaurant have a two-way mirror? That seemed a little far-fetched, but no more so than the evening had been thus far.

Our waiter appeared behind me with a bottle of wine, opened it, and set the cork down for me. I picked it up and took a whiff. "Smells good." I looked up at him, detecting a slight roll of his eyes.

He poured a small amount into my wineglass and handed it to me to taste. Mattie and I frequently had wine at home but not in this class. "Very nice."

He poured me a full glass, then one across the table before leaving the bottle, prompting a "Thank you, Eduardo" this time. *Is he on a first-name basis with the entire wait staff? He must come here weekly.*

I was tempted to ask, but I had already decided on a different strategy. I leaned back in my chair and turned to "Jesus," suppressing my customary sarcastic smile. "So your family called you Yeshua?"

"Most of them. James called me a few other things."

"Well, Yesh— Do you mind if I call you Yesh?"

"Whatever suits you."

"Yesh it is, then. Tell me,"—I held up my wineglass— "can you turn this wine back into water?"

3

The Menu

"NO PROBLEM," HE replied. He turned and signaled for the waiter, who came to the table. "My friend would like a second glass of water instead of this wine."

With a "Certainly, sir," the waiter removed my wineglass and turned to retrieve water.

"Very funny," I muttered before calling after the waiter. "I think I'll keep my wine."

"Very well, sir." He returned the glass to the table.

"Thank you, Eduardo," my host said. "Sorry to bother you."

Eduardo departed. I opened my menu and momentarily buried myself in it. The quality of the dinner conversation was doubtful, but not the caliber of the food. Guests selected a four-course meal: an appetizer, a salad, an entrée, and later a dessert. I gave half of my attention to my order, the other half to contemplating what I was still doing here. My growling stomach answered that question; I had worked straight through lunch.

"What do you think?"

I lowered my menu enough to peek over it. "I think I'm crazy for not leaving when I had the chance."

"About your order."

Last time we came Mattie ordered something really good. What was it?

"The veal," I finally responded. I plopped the menu down, emphasizing my one accomplishment so far that night—deciding what to eat.

"I'll go with the salmon."

"Is this a Friday?"

A slight smile curled his lips. "Touché," he said.

He placed his menu on the table, and the waiter appeared immediately.

"Are you ready to order, sir?" he asked me.

"Yes. I'll take the stuffed mushrooms, the Mediterranean salad, and veal fantarella."

"Certainly." He turned to my dinner partner. "And you, sir?"

"I would like the tomato and artichoke soup, the tortellini salad, and the salmon filet, please."

An upgrade from his usual bread and wine, to say the least.

As the waiter walked off with our menus, "Jesus" leaned

back in his chair, took a sip of wine, and made a first stab at initiating real conversation. "Tell me about your family."

"I thought you knew everything already." I dodged the question. "You had Judas figured out. Didn't help you much, if I may say so."

He probably assumed I didn't know anything about religion or the Bible, but I'd served my time in Sunday school. I'd hated every minute of it, of course. After Mother drove Dad away, she used to take Ellen, Chelle, and me to church. She'd tell us, "We need a good influence, for once." Stacy, sixteen by then, refused to go. I should have too, but being younger, I wielded limited power.

So I went. The lessons served as background noise to the real activities of passing notes, throwing spit wads at the girls, and stealing from the "junior" collection plate. The teachers were mostly nondescript—a few men who wore pasted-on smiles, trying to make it seem as though they actually wanted to be there, and women who thought that boys actually enjoyed flannelboard Bible stories.

One lady, Mrs. Willard, was a classic. Her mantra was "love one another as yourself." Yet the minute someone so much as twitched an eyebrow, she'd grab him by the ear, drag him to the front, and make him write a hundred "I will do unto others as I would have them do unto me." Maybe that's what she did want others to do unto her.

I learned little by example at church, but a few Bible stories did seep through: the Good Samaritan, the Bad Samaritan,
the Mediocre Samaritan. I'd caught enough to keep up with
this guy for a while.

"Why don't you humor me?" he answered, ignoring my
Judas reference. "Where is your family from?"

I wasn't about to let him off the hook that easily. After all,
he was the one claiming to be Jesus. Now he had to play the
part.

"I'm much more interested in your family, Yesh." I felt a
smirk creep onto my face. "Tell me about Joseph and Mary."

He jumped right in. "Growing up in Nazareth wasn't
exactly like boyhood in Chicago. We didn't go for foot-long
hot dogs and Cracker Jacks at Wrigley."

"Oh, really?" I responded sarcastically. What I didn't say
was, *Funny he picked Chicago, and Wrigley Field, where Dad
and I went every Saturday.*

He continued. "Joseph was a good father. He had to
work a lot, but it wasn't like today. His shop next to the house
had an unhurried pace. Joseph only sped up when he heard
me coming. He always tried to finish a project before I could
get my hands on it."

He put his hand on his chin, looked away, and laughed. "I
didn't realize at the time how many of his pieces I used to mess

up. He'd be making a table or something, and I'd want to help. Needless to say, at eight I wasn't exactly a master carpenter. He'd go back and redo some from scratch that I had 'helped' on. Other pieces he'd go ahead and use. Some of the neighbors kindly accepted items that had my unique imprint."

Half of me listened to this spiel; the other half analyzed him. The guys must have hired a professional actor for this part. He actually talked like he had grown up in Nazareth. This guy was *good*.

I was going to ask about Mary when the waiter appeared with a loaf of hot bread and some spinach spread. "Jesus" reached for the bread knife, cut a slice, and held the board toward me.

"Some bread?"

I took the slice and tried some of the spread before proceeding with the family history. "So Joseph was just a regular Joe. And Mary—it must have been rough growing up with such a revered mom."

He chuckled, either slightly amused or annoyed—I couldn't tell which. "She was hardly revered. More like an outcast when I was young. Having a child before the wedding was not—"

"Kosher," I interjected, trying to get in the Jewish spirit of things.

He paused. "It wasn't the thing to do."

"From all the paintings it seems like Mary was always either seeing angels or nursing you or taking you off the cross. Did she do anything in between?"

The question was a bit over the top, I guess. But I had to do something to rock this guy out of his routine. He acted way too natural. Even this didn't faze him, though. He just took some more bread and went on talking.

"I had a great mother. Her faith kept her going—and her sense of humor. She never let me live down my remark as a kid that I had to be about my Father's business. Someone would come to our house looking for me. 'I don't know where he is,' she would say. 'About his Father's business.' The older I got, the more she would say, 'Do you think your Father's business might involve finding a girl and settling down?'"

A smile crossed his face as he talked. He paused, then got more serious. "When I finally started preaching, it got hard for her, seeing her son worshiped one day and demonized the next. It was harder for her than she expected."

Maybe she should have gone on Dr. Phil's show. He probably could have helped her out. I was finding this routine a little wearing.

"Look, you haven't told me anything that someone with

a Bible and half an imagination couldn't make up. You're going to have to come up with something better than these sappy Joseph and Mary stories."

"To do what?" he asked.

That was a good question. What exactly did I expect from a guy pretending to be Jesus? I guess something a little more interesting. Larry King once said that of all the personalities in history, he would most like to have interviewed Jesus. Talking with Jesus Christ—or even his impostor—should have been more engaging than this. Surely this guy had something in mind other than rehashing old Bible stories.

His voice snapped me back to the conversation. "I don't think there's much I can say that would actually convince you I'm Jesus."

"Well, that's one true statement."

"I have a suggestion. Why don't you suspend your disbelief for a while and proceed as if I am Jesus? Surely if Jesus were actually here, you might have some questions for him."

That wasn't a bad idea. We were getting nowhere with my trying to figure out his real identity. And this had the potential to be interesting. Assuming this guy knew his stuff, this might be the best philosophical discussion I'd had since...Northern Illinois days? We actually used to talk about Kant and Kierkegaard and even Feynman back then.

The closest thing I got to that now were those ridiculous parenting books that Mattie force-fed me.

"Okay, fine," I replied. "I have one for you. The other day I passed by the church down the street, and their sign read, '"No one comes to the Father but through me"— Jesus.' If you actually said that, I think you're full of it."

4

The Appetizer

"YOUR TOMATO AND artichoke soup, sir."

I cringed. The waiter's intrusion had ruined the whole setup. I had just landed my first blow, had this fraud reeling, when the interruption gave him time to regroup. His dish was served first. Then Eduardo brought mine around and set a plate in front of me.

"Your stuffed mushrooms."

I looked across the table where "Jesus" sat, making no move toward his utensils. *Oh, great. Now what's he going to do—ask me to say grace?*

"I usually say a short word of thanks before meals. Do you mind?"

"Whatever" was my preferred response, but "No, not at all" was what came out.

He raised his head toward the ceiling and left his eyes

open. I couldn't help but follow his gaze, wondering if I had missed something up there. I hadn't.

"Father, thank you for always providing for us, whom you love." He lowered his head, took a spoon in his hand, and dipped into his soup.

"That's it?" I asked.

"Is there something else you would like to say?"

"No. No, I guess that covers it." I grabbed a fork and speared one of the mushrooms.

We sat silently for a number of moments, eating our appetizers. I debated how to circle back to my question when my host solved the problem for me.

"Why do you think I'm mistaken?" he asked.

"Because here you've got all these people around the world who believe in all these different things and worship God in all these different ways, and Jesus claimed only his way was the right one?"

"And your difficulty with that is…"

"A lot. Who is to say that Jesus's way was any better than Muhammad's or Buddha's or Confucius's or… Well, there really wasn't a specific Hindu guy." *Did he pick up on the fact that I knew which religions had a founder and which did not?*

"Do you think Hinduism is true?" he inquired.

"I don't know. My friends Dave and Paula have gotten into some Hindu stuff, and it seems to work for them."

He reached for another piece of bread and applied some spinach spread. "I didn't ask if you thought it worked. I asked if you thought it was true."

"Well, it's true for them."

He took a bite of his bread and seemed to ponder how to respond. "Before Copernicus, most people believed the earth was flat. That was false, but it worked for them. Why?"

"I suppose it didn't matter much back then. Until Columbus, they never traveled far enough for it to be a problem. Well, except for the Vikings."

"And what if humanity had tried to go to the moon while still believing the earth was flat?"

"So you're saying…"

"What people believed worked for them, to a point, even though it wasn't true. But at some critical juncture it ceased to work anymore."

"And…"

"You tell me. You're the one with the master's degree."

"In business, not philosophy."

"You had to think a little." He reached for his spoon.

I wasn't sure how I'd gotten off the offensive and was now playing near my own goal line, but I decided I might as well go along. Besides, I admit I was starting to find the conversation a tad intriguing. "What you're saying is that even if a belief system seems to work for someone, if it's false, eventually it will break down."

He leaned forward. "And you don't want what you're ultimately trusting to be wrong." He paused a moment, then leapfrogged forward. "Now, you're the scientist."

"Used to be."

"And you took that comparative religion class at Northern Illinois. What do you think? How does Hinduism line up with what you know about the universe?"

"How did you—," I started to respond. *But what's the point? He seems to have this whole scene, including me, thoroughly researched. I just hope there's a limit to what he's found out.* I returned to the question. "As I recall, Hinduism teaches that the universe is simply an extension of this universal force called…"

"Brahman."

"Yeah, Brahman, the ultimate essence."

"So God is the universe, and the universe is God."

"Right. There is no separate creator."

He slid back in his chair. "And how long has the universe existed?"

"Well, some Hindus would say always. Brahman is eternal, so the universe is eternal."

"How does that match what your astronomers have discovered in the last century?"

I pondered that one for a moment. "Not too well," I admitted. Although I had loved cosmology in college (I would have majored in astronomy if I could have made any money at it), I hadn't thought down this path before. "All the evidence points to the fact that the universe had an actual beginning in time, maybe fifteen billion years ago."

"What if that number is wrong?"

"The universe still can't be eternal. The second law of thermodynamics. In a closed system, everything eventually winds down. In an infinitely old universe, we wouldn't see new stars or galaxies forming. It all would have wound down, with no productive energy remaining. A couple of people, like Hoyle, tried to hold on to the steady-state theory, in which the universe would be eternal, but no one accepts it anymore."

"Jesus" leaned forward and entwined his fingers on the table. "So if Hinduism is true, how did the universe get here?"

"I don't know."

He smiled. "I don't know, either."

We took a couple of bites before he spoke again. "Hinduism's depiction of reality has other problems."

"Like what?"

"Morality, for one. Humans are highly moral beings. All societies, even primitive ones, have complex—and similar—moral codes."

"Agreed."

"Now, let me ask you this: what is the ultimate source of morality in Hinduism? Does Brahman establish right and wrong?"

I picked a piece of bread off my plate and thought about that one a second. "No, Brahman is amoral. With the universal force, nothing is ultimately right or wrong. It simply is."

"So what is the basis of morality if the source of all things is nonmoral? What makes anything inherently right or wrong?"

"We do, I suppose."

"But you are an extension of Brahman, which is amoral."

I didn't have a reply to that one. He continued. "Hinduism has a similar issue with personality. One of the things people appreciate most about themselves is their individuality. It's part of what it means to be human. Do you remember what Hinduism teaches about that?"

"Yeah. Personality is an illusion. You have to renounce it to enter into oneness with the universe."

"So what you most value about yourself is illusory. One

day you'll be reabsorbed into Brahman and lose your individuality."

I had to admit, that never had sounded all that appealing.

"If personality is an illusion," he asked, "why are people all so individual? How did an impersonal universal force bring forth such unique personalities?"

"But you could make these arguments about all Eastern religions."

"Yes. That's the problem with them. The world is not as they describe. They provide a way of understanding life, but it's a false understanding." He leaned back, wiping his mouth. "What do you remember about Buddhism?"

Buddhism was always a little easier to get a handle on than Hinduism. It was hard to forget the Four Noble Truths and the Eightfold Path. I couldn't name them all, but I did remember the main idea.

"Buddhism is kind of like Hinduism in its basic worldview," I said. "Ultimate reality is this…abstract void called nirvana. You enter nirvana by traveling an Eightfold Path and stamping out all attachment or desire in yourself. Once you've eliminated that, all your suffering ends."

He picked up his wineglass and held it in front of him, looking at the wine and then peering at me through the glass with a strangely distorted face. He moved the glass to the side of his vision. "Someone made this glass well. They were attached to a sense of fine craftsmanship."

"Probably."

"How much have humans accomplished without someone having passion?"

"Not much," I conceded.

"You've taken plenty of biology. How many sensory nerve cells do we have in our skin, capable of providing pleasure?"

"Millions."

"So somehow an impersonal universe has taken the form of personal beings with strong desires and the ability to feel great pleasure, and yet the goal of life is to negate all desire." He put the glass down.

"I suppose it doesn't make much sense," I said, making his point for him.

"Do you think that perhaps suffering was so great in India that Siddhartha Gautama, the Buddha, tried to come up with some explanation for it and developed an entire belief system based on alleviating suffering?"

My answer, or lack thereof, was preempted by the waiter appearing on my right. "Are you finished with your mushrooms, sir?"

I momentarily considered the two that remained. "Sure."

He removed our dishes, a well-timed interruption. Too much more talk about Eastern religions and my ignorance would start showing. One thing was certain. I wasn't going to play this guy in Trivial Pursuit, Religion Edition. At the risk of getting in over my head, I wanted to see what he would say about something closer to Christianity.

"What about Islam?" I asked. "Maybe pantheistic religions don't hold up. But Muslims claim to worship the God of the Bible. Who says that their version is wrong and Jesus was right?"

He reached for his water, then answered. "That depends on whether God actually spoke to Muhammad, doesn't it? That's a lot of weight to give one guy's writings, especially one who, after supposedly hearing from an angel, wasn't sure whether he had heard from God, had persistent bouts of suicidal thoughts, built a following based partly on military conquest, countenanced the murder of his enemies, and married a nine-year-old, among other things."

"Who says that? I've never heard those things, except the military part."

"Revered Muslim writings. The *Sirat Rasul Allah*. The Hadith collections of Bukhari, Muslim, and Abu Dawud. *The History of al-Tabari,* among others."

I didn't have any basis on which to argue the point with

him, so I returned to his original statement. "But you could say the same about Christianity, that it revolves around whether God spoke to some guy."

"No, the Bible has over forty authors spanning fifteen hundred years, all with a consistent message. That argues for, not against, a divine origin."

"Still, who's to say that God didn't speak to Muhammad?"

"If God did, he got some things wrong."

"Like what?"

"Muhammad wrote that I was never crucified, that God's angels rescued me and took me straight to heaven."

"You mean Jesus."

"That's what I said."

I decided not to rehash that debate. "So maybe Muhammad was right."

That elicited a slight smile. "No, he wasn't."

"Oh, of course. I forgot. You were there."

"But you don't have to ask me," he continued, ignoring my comment. "My crucifixion is historically documented, not only by early Christians, but also by non-Christian historians of the time. Throw it out, and you have to throw out everything you know about ancient history."

I couldn't disagree, actually. You could debate about the resurrection, but Jesus's crucifixion was a certainty. I was about to ask another question when he resumed.

"Islam teaches other things that aren't true."

"Such as?"

"That the Bible has been altered over time so that what you have now is a highly corrupted version that can't be trusted."

"So?"

"So that's false. Any scholar in the field will tell you that. The Dead Sea Scrolls, among other things, prove the reliability of the Hebrew Bible. And you have over five thousand early manuscripts that validate the New Testament. You have what the authors wrote. It's up to you what to do with it, but you have what they wrote."

He moved his wineglass toward the top of his place setting. "But that's not the biggest problem with Islam."

"Which is…"

He looked around the room for a second, scanning for I'm not sure what. His eyes returned to me. "What is your deepest desire?"

Where did that question come from? "I'm not sure I want to get into that."

"Then let's talk in generalities. What do people in their hearts most deeply long for?"

"A raise?" I kidded. All right, half kidded. He didn't respond.

I thought for a minute, glancing around the room

myself. The ravioli guy and his girl were still making cow eyes at each other across their cleared table. "I suppose people's greatest desire is to be loved." I looked back at my host.

He leaned forward, and his voice softened. "I don't mean to be too personal, Nick. But in your experience, has another person ever fulfilled your need for love?"

He is getting too personal, whether he wants to or not. Besides, I thought we were talking about Islam. I resisted the urge to look away again, though I did shift back in my chair. I thought of my dad, of Mattie, of Elizabeth, my girlfriend at NIU. "No, not really."

"That's because another person can never satisfy it. Only God can. He designed people that way. But Muslims never have that hope. You can't have a personal relationship with Allah. He is someone to worship and serve from afar, even in paradise. It doesn't meet the deepest need of humanity's heart. Why would God create humanity with this deep need, then never meet it?"

I kept my eyes on him for a moment, then picked up my wineglass and took a drink. "Maybe Muslims don't have all the answers. But I don't think anybody does."

"No, they don't. They only think they do."

He spoke not sarcastically or arrogantly but with almost a hint of sadness. Uncomfortable with the subsequent silence, I glanced toward the river but saw in the window only the reflection of my face and the back of his head.

"What if God doesn't even exist?" I looked back toward him. "Maybe the material world is all there is."

"Then you have the problem of design."

"What, that there's no way it could have happened by accident?" It was a common argument and, frankly, a good one.

"You're aware of Roger Penrose," he said.

"Yeah. Helped develop black hole theory."

"Do you know the odds he calculated of a cosmic accident producing this orderly universe rather than chaos?"

I hadn't read Penrose's calculation, but I had seen similar comments by Hawking, Dyson, and others. I guessed: "One in a million?"

"Try one in a hundred billion, to the one hundred twenty-third power."

"Not very good odds."

"And that's just the macrouniverse. He omits the design complexity of biological life."

He had me there. The more I'd studied cosmology, the more apparent the design in the universe had become. I thought those who promoted the idea of random chance had more of a philosophical ax to grind than science on their side.

I reached for a piece of bread, spread butter on it this

time, and took a bite. "Okay, fine. I agree that there has to be some transcendent being, not just physical existence. And you're great at poking holes in all these other religions. But it seems to me that all religions, including Christianity, are different paths to the same place. I mean, everyone is looking for God, and—"

"Are you?"

That interjection caught me by surprise. *Am I looking for God? You wouldn't think so, observing my life.* I decided to ignore his question.

"As I was saying, it seems like everyone is looking for God in their own way. That's what I like about the church our friends Dave and Paula attend. They embrace everyone's beliefs and try to help them on their path to God."

"There's one problem with that thinking," he said.

"What?"

"There is no path to God."

That was the last thing I expected to hear.

5

The Salad

To my right, the waiter lingered with our salads, for how long I don't know. Our pause cued his approach. Maybe he avoided interrupting "serious" conversations. I guess this one qualified. I wasn't quite sure how I got suckered into a God discussion, but it was more captivating than my college prof pontificating on comparative religion. Mr. Drone, we called him, for his preferred lecture style.

The tortellini salad across the table jogged my memory. *That was what Mattie had ordered that was so good. Oh, well.* I pulled my selection closer and reached for a new fork.

"Care for some tortellini?" my host asked, pointing to his own salad. Before I had a chance to respond, he reached over, grabbed my empty bread plate, scooped half of his portion onto it, and handed it to me.

"That's too much," I said in polite protest.

"This place serves enough food for two dinners. I have plenty."

He was right about the servings, and I wasn't about to argue. I took the dish and pushed my own salad to the side. "Thank you."

I took a bite. "This is ungodly."

He tasted it as well but didn't respond. I had a couple more bites before getting the conversation back on track.

"What do you mean, there's no path to God? Every religion claims to teach the way to God."

"Oh, there's a way to God," he said. "Just not a path."

He had lost me. From the look on my face, he probably knew it.

"What I mean is this: a path is something you travel down by your own effort to reach a destination. But there's no such path to God. There is nothing you can do to work your way to God. That path doesn't exist. It—"

"Wait a minute. That's what all religion is about, trying to get to God. How can you say otherwise?"

He took another couple of bites before responding. "Did you ever get into trouble as a kid?"

"Are we changing the subject?"

"We'll get back to the other."

I wasn't too sure I wanted to talk about me anymore, although in truth it was a favorite subject of mine. "I don't think this place stays open late enough for all my trouble-making history."

He smiled. "That bad? Give me a highlight."

I reached over to sample my own salad. My mind raced from getting my first spanking to playing Halloween pranks to teasing my sister Ellen to aborting a plan to smoke bomb the high-school teachers' lounge to… *No point in bringing up the present.* I backtracked.

"When I was four, my mother made these Christmas decorations—miniature drummer-boy drums. I don't know what she used them for. Anyway, she'd covered the sides with green and red crepe paper, plus somehow she had attached spearmint Life Savers on the sides."

He started smiling, probably knowing where this was heading.

"So she had them in the utility room, on the washer and dryer. And I snuck in there and plucked a Life Saver off one of the drums. Then I crossed through the kitchen, where Mother was, to get out. But a few minutes later I went back in, saying, 'I forgot something' as I entered the utility room. When I tried it a third time, my 'I forgot something again' wasn't too convincing."

I started chuckling to myself. "She opened the door, and there I was, stuffing my pockets with as many Life Savers as I could. That was the first spanking I remember. Actually, my dad did it when he got home. He always used to do it. He wasn't too mad, really. But Mother was, so he had to."

I paused, lost momentarily in my childhood. "Once Dad got really mad, though."

"When…"

"When I was about nine. My sister Chelle must've been five. We had stopped at a burger place for some ice cream, and Chelle wanted a big vanilla shake. Dad tried to talk her into a small one, but she insisted on a large. So we all got our orders, got back in the car, and drove off. Then Chelle started on her shake. But the thing was so thick that she couldn't use a straw. So she took the plastic top off and tilted it toward her mouth. Except it was barely moving, and she kept tilting it up farther and farther, and the main blob still wasn't moving. So finally I said, 'Come on, Chelle!' and reached over and gave the bottom of the cup a *whap*. When I did that, the whole thing came cascading onto her face. When she opened her eyes, all you could see were these two big, brown circles poking out through the white ice cream."

He started laughing with me. I continued. "She looked like a ghost. I burst out laughing, she burst out crying, and my dad burst out yelling—at me. He never used to do that, but this time he did. He slammed on the brakes, got out, wiped her off as best he could, then bent me over his knee and gave me my worst spanking ever. He was not happy."

I wiped my eyes with my napkin. I hadn't thought about that in years or laughed so hard in a while, either. "I think that was the last vanilla shake I ever saw Chelle get. She always ordered chocolate after that."

We both took a drink of water, looked at each other, and chuckled a bit more as we returned to our salads. Finally he got us back to semiserious conversation. "So your dad always handled the spanking."

"Yeah. Mother just screamed at us. But Dad didn't spank much. I probably didn't get half a dozen spankings growing up."

"Why not?"

"I don't know." I thought about that for a second. "I don't know. That just wasn't his way of handling things. Usually he made sure we understood why what we had done was wrong. Then he always made us apologize to the other person. Especially to Mother."

I took another bite of tortellini. He had a sip of wine, then said, "It sounds as though your dad had a lot in common with God."

That one cut short my next bite en route to my mouth. "How so?"

"They both focused on restoring relationships."

I wasn't quite getting the connection. "Meaning…"

"Your dad had you admit how you had hurt someone

and apologize. He was interested in restoring relationships."

I guess that's true. I've never thought about it that way.

"God is like that," he continued. "He's not interested in people trying to perform well enough for him. They can't. He created people to have a relationship with him, to enjoy his love. But humanity rejected God and severed that relationship. His program is putting it back together."

He paused, took a bite, then gestured with his fork toward me. "Let me ask you this. When Sara is seven and she does something wrong, how many dishes will she have to wash before she can sit in your lap and have you hug her again?"

"None."

"How many A's will she have to make in school?"

"That's ridiculous."

"Why?"

"She won't have to do anything. She's my daughter."

"Exactly."

I looked down and sampled some more of my salad, letting that sink in. Finally my gaze returned to him. "You're saying that we can't do anything to earn God's acceptance."

He smiled and reached for the wine bottle. "A little more?"

"Sure."

He poured me half a glass. My mind was still racing from his last statement—or my summation. He proceeded.

"Muslims who try to earn their way into paradise—how many daily prayers do they have to perform to be good enough?"

"I don't know."

"Neither do they. That's the problem. They can never be sure if they've done enough—enough praying, fasting, giving to the poor, making pilgrimages. They can never know. Ask them, and they will admit that. Hindus can never know how many hundreds of lifetimes it may take to successfully work out their karma. Buddhists can never know how much effort it will take to reach nirvana."

"But Christianity is no different," I responded. "No one can ever know if he has really been good enough to make it to heaven."

"Oh, people can know that for certain. The answer is, they haven't been. No one is good enough to make it to heaven. No one can ever be good enough, no matter how hard they try."

"But what about all the people who think that going to church or giving money or being a good person will get them into heaven? Mrs. Willard, my Sunday school teacher, sure thought that would get people in."

"She was wrong. It won't."

This was stretching my concept of Christianity. "So you're saying that doing all the right things, like keeping the Ten Commandments, won't get you into heaven?"

"Correct."

"Then why do them?"

"There's great profit in obeying God. It just won't get you into heaven."

For a moment I didn't know what to say. *How can this guy say something so different from what I heard in church growing up?* Maybe he realized my predicament, because he resumed the conversation.

"You're a *Star Trek* fan."

I didn't know where he got his information, and I had decided to stop asking. "I liked *The Next Generation.* I never got into the follow-ups much."

"There's an episode where they talk about a rift, a tear, in the fabric of space-time. It's a huge problem. The galaxy will be destroyed if they don't repair it."

"Something tells me we're not going to start talking about *Star Trek.*"

"Maybe not," he replied. "But it's a great illustration. There is a moral fabric to the universe. Humanity's rebellion against God is a massive rip in that fabric. It's an overthrow of the entire way God designed the universe to operate. Every person's sin tears this moral fabric."

It was hard to deny that humanity is pretty screwed up. The evening news proved that.

"But who is to say that humanity isn't evolving spiritually? Like Dave and Paula say, maybe we're all moving toward a greater universal harmony." I had to admit I wasn't too convinced myself, but it was worth considering. Momentarily, at least.

"Humanity's separation from God is much more profound than people realize. Just look around. The selfishness, bitterness, hatred, prejudice, exploitation, abuse, wars—all these result from humanity's rebellion against God. Do you think God designed people to operate this way?"

"But some of those things are getting better," I chimed in optimistically.

"Really?" His eyebrows rose. "How many people were murdered by their own governments in the last century?"

"Oh, I dunno," I replied. "A hundred million or so."

"And how many killed in wars?"

"Probably about the same."

"In what century have the most people been killed for their faith?"

"Let me guess. The last one?"

"Right. And in what century do you think there has been more ecological damage, exploitation of the world's poor, rampant immorality—"

"Okay, you've made your point," I said, halting the litany of human ills.

"There's a rip in the fabric of the universe," he repeated. "God stands on one side of the tear; you stand on the other. And there's no way for you to repair it. There's no way at all to the other side. Trying to be good enough is irrelevant. Humanity rejected God, separated itself from him, and can't do anything to reestablish that relationship."

"Why not?"

"Because only God is big enough to fix the tear."

I had a feeling he was going to say that.

6

The Main Course

THE PROBLEM WITH places like Milano's is that by the time the main course arrives, you're stuffed. Well, not completely stuffed, but at a point where you wouldn't consider ordering veal fantarella with grilled vegetables. Of course, when the veal comes, and you take your first bite, room magically reappears in your belly.

I had been stuffed with God talk years ago, and I still felt the need for a good purge. But here I was, forty minutes into this dinner, and I hadn't reached my fill. I'm not sure why. To be honest, this guy both intrigued and baffled me. There he sat, one minute eating his salmon as if this dinner was the most natural thing in the world, the next saying stuff about God I'm certain I never heard in Sunday school.

"Do you have something to write on?" He took a pen from his coat pocket.

I pulled out my wallet and searched through it. "Not really. A couple of receipts. A business card."

"That'll do."

I turned it to the blank side and handed it to him. He continued. "Who is the best person you can think of?"

"What do you mean?"

"Morally speaking. Who is the best?"

"I don't know." I thought for a moment. "Living or dead?"

"Either."

"Mother Teresa maybe. She had a fairly good reputation."

"Okay." He drew a short line near the top of the card and put "Mother Teresa" next to it. "Who is the worst?"

"Well, Osama bin Laden turned out pretty bad, but there have been worse. Hitler. Stalin. Pol Pot."

"Pick one."

"Hitler."

He marked a line near the bottom and wrote "Hitler" next to it. Turning the card around toward me, he offered me the pen. I took it from him. "Now, Mother Teresa is at the top. Hitler is at the bottom. Where do you think you fall on this scale?"

The busboy appeared behind my companion and filled his water glass. I let the conversation pause while he came around and filled mine. He left, and I returned to the question at hand. "How can anyone answer that? If you put yourself closer to Mother Teresa, you look vain. If you put yourself closer to Hitler…" I let that speak for itself.

"So where do you think?" he asked, unmoved by my dilemma.

I raised the pen. "Here." I drew a mark above the middle, somewhat closer to Mother Teresa. "So what do I win?"

"Nothing. But I will tell you how you stack up in God's eyes."

"Okay." At least, that's what I said. I wasn't really sure I wanted to hear my score.

"Actually, this business card doesn't constitute the entire scale. Hitler is here." He pointed at the bottom. "You say you are here, and Mother Teresa is here. But to get a feel for how high God's actual standard is"—he stood the card on its end—"imagine that we went to Chicago and put this card at the base of the Sears Tower. God's moral standard is the top of the tower, over one hundred stories up."

"Are you saying that to God, Mother Teresa and Hitler are essentially the same?"

"Oh no. Hitler was horribly evil. Mother Teresa did very much good. It is not the same. But the point is this: Mother Teresa, in her own goodness, is no closer to bridging the gap to God than Hitler is. They are both sinners, and both on their own merits are separated from God."

I thought about that for a few seconds before responding. "So you're saying that no one can make it."

"Not on their own merit. No one is even close. <u>God's standard is perfection.</u> And you wouldn't want it any other way."

I was still thinking about the implications of his prior statement; this new one took a second to register. "I'm sorry. What? What do you mean, I wouldn't want it any other way?"

"You wouldn't want the universe run by someone who wasn't perfectly holy and perfectly just."

"Why not?" *Perfect holiness is the last thing I need to deal with.*

"Because it would offend your God-given sense of justice. Would you want a universe where crime went unpunished? Where, if someone harmed Sara, there'd be no justice? Where evil reigned unopposed? God has to punish sin, because if he doesn't, he lets all creation be sabotaged. How would it have been if, after the Holocaust, God had said to Hitler, 'That's okay, Adolf. We all make mistakes. Don't worry about it'?"

"But everyone isn't Hitler!"

"No, but everyone is a rebel against God. It doesn't take horrific outward acts. For the universe, <u>humanity's rebellion is more like cancer than like a heart attack.</u> It isn't mass murder that destroys the world. It's selfishness, resentment, envy, pride—all the daily sins of the heart. God has to deal with the cancer."

"But we've all felt those things. We're human."

"Yes."

I waited for more, but he returned to his salmon. The import of what he had said slowly sank in. "It just doesn't seem right that God sees everyone the same way. Some people are worse than others."

"And God will judge them all rightly. But that's the point. Everyone is already under God's judgment, because everyone has violated his moral law. On what basis are you going to stand before a perfectly holy God and say that you've been good enough?"

I picked up my fork to stab another piece of veal, then put it down again and reached for some water. Suddenly the conversation unsettled me.

"You read *Lord of the Flies*," he resumed, "about the shipwrecked English boys who created their own society and ended up brutalizing each other."

"Yeah."

"Why did they come to accept such brutality as normal?"

"They were cut off from civilization. I suppose they gradually forgot what was right. At least, it got all mixed up for them."

He nodded. "It did. They lacked a compass to guide their behavior. Humanity is the same way. People are cut off from God, so they've lost a sense of how abhorrent sin really is. They live in a sinful world, and it almost seems normal. But to God it is grotesque. God is holy and just, in an absolute sense. Humanity doesn't have any point of comparison with that. That's why people continually try to water down God's holiness. The way Islam does."

My ears perked up on that one. "Like Islam? If there's one thing Muslims emphasize, it's God's justice and his punishment of wickedness."

"That's what they claim. But ask them what happens on the judgment day. They say that if you've done enough good deeds, Allah will overlook your bad ones, and you'll get into paradise."

"So?"

"So Allah has to deny perfect justice in order to be merciful. There's no penalty for wrongdoing if you have done enough good things to offset it. But true justice doesn't work that way, not even on earth. If someone is convicted of fraud, the judge doesn't say, 'Well, he was a kind Little League coach. That offsets it.' In Islam, Allah is not perfectly just, because if he were, people would have to pay the penalty for every sin, and no one would get into paradise. That's what perfect justice is."

I pushed the vegetables around on my neglected plate. "But I thought God is forgiving. You're implying that because of justice, God can't forgive."

"God is forgiving. God wants to forgive people more than anything in the world, to restore them to himself. What I'm saying is that God's desire to forgive doesn't negate his perfect justice. Someone has to pay the penalty for sins. God's justice demands it."

This seemed like a Catch-22 of the worst kind. I reached for a piece of bread, mostly to buy time to think. He finished off his salmon, apparently content to let me formulate my next question.

"So what has to happen to get us back to God?"

"God had two options. He could let people pay for their own sins..."

"Resulting in..."

"Humanity being separated from him forever."

"That's not a good one. What was the other option?"

"Or God could pay the penalty himself."

"How?"

"He is God. The Creator is greater than the creation. For the Creator to take the penalty of death himself, instead of those he created, satisfies perfect justice."

"Why would God do that?"

He reached for his water. "Let me ask you something.

Imagine that Sara is seventeen, and she falls in with a bad crowd and gets hooked on heroin."

"That's a little bleak, don't you think?"

"Just hypothetically. Now, if while on drugs, she murdered someone and was sentenced to death, would you take her penalty if you could?"

That was a hard one. Needless to say, I hadn't exactly pondered it before. But...

"I'm sure I would."

"Why?"

"Because I love her. And she would have the rest of her life, and I would want to give her the chance to make it a good one."

He leaned toward me, moved his plate forward, and rested his forearms against the table. "Don't you think God loves you at least as much as you love Sara?"

I shifted back in my chair, but my eyes never left his. "Maybe. I really don't know."

He leaned back himself. "I heard about two boys in fifth grade. One of them made straight A's; the other barely passed every year. Despite their different grades, they were best friends—had been since kindergarten.

"Near the end of the school year, they had a big math test. The first boy sailed through it; the second, who needed to make a C to pass, struggled. After class, the first asked the second how he did. 'I don't think I made it,' he said. That day at recess, while everyone played outside, the first boy sneaked back into the classroom, shuffled through the stack of tests, and found their two. He erased his name on his and wrote his friend's name there and then wrote his name on his friend's."

I waited for a second, but he seemed to be finished. "That's all?"

"What else were you expecting?"

"Well, the story's not over. When the teacher returned and graded the papers, she would have known what he did."

"No. The story ends there. What does it tell you?"

"That the first kid was willing to exchange his grade so that his friend could pass."

"Yes, and more than that." He ran his hand across his chin. "What would have happened if the second kid had failed?"

"He would have been held back the next year probably."

"And then…"

"They couldn't have gone through school together anymore."

He paused for a moment, then spoke a little more softly. "God longs to have you with him. That's why he created you. But your sin separates you from him. It has to, if God is just. You have to be innocent before God. So, to get you back,

God took your sin upon himself, and he died to pay for it. That satisfies his justice. In exchange, he offers you a not-guilty verdict. He offers it as a free gift."

I wasn't entirely sure about this alleged gift, which sounded too good to be true, but I had to ask the logical question. "What do you have to do to get it?"

"Just receive it. That's all."

"You don't have to do anything for it?"

"No."

"And how do you receive it?"

"Just trust him. That's what all relationships are built on: trust. You reestablish a relationship with God by trusting that he died to pay for your sins. Believe that he will forgive your sins and give you eternal life. That's why he died for you. He wants you back. All you have to do is accept the gift."

I wanted to look away, but my eyes seemed frozen. I wasn't convinced that God loved me all that much, and I sure didn't know if I wanted him. And this last statement confused me.

"I don't get it. The Bible says that Jesus died on the cross, not God."

"Nick," he replied, "I am God."

7

The Dessert

"EXCUSE ME A minute, would you?"

I stood and headed toward the men's room. Passing the lattice, I hooked a right and entered the bathroom. I took care of business, stepped to the sink, and looked at myself in the mirror.

Now what?

It's not every day that someone tells you he's God. Maybe if you worked in a psych ward—I don't know.

This guy is either a nut or a really good actor or…

I dismissed the last possibility. *But why would anyone want to put on this show? What would be the point—to bamboozle me "into the kingdom"? Who would do that? Okay, I can think of a few televangelists who might, but this guy doesn't come off that way. I can't refute anything he's said. I don't necessarily agree with it all, but it's not off the wall. Except that last statement.*

I splashed my face with water, dried off, and headed back toward the table, unsure what to do. I considered taking a right at the lattice and going straight for the parking lot, but something stopped me. I couldn't help wanting to know more about this guy who claimed to be...

I returned to the table. Our plates had been replaced by dessert menus.

"The waiter recommends the strawberry amaretto cake."

He looked over his menu. I stared at him, waiting for him to put it down and look up at me. He finally did.

"Prove it."

"Prove..."

"That you're God."

"What would convince you?"

Good question. What could anyone possibly do to convince you of that?

"You couldn't even turn wine into water earlier."

"That's your assumption."

"What?! Are you saying you could have but just chose not to?"

"And what if I had changed it?"

"Well, it might have gotten my attention."

"And then what?"

Another good question. It's not like he doesn't have my attention sufficiently.

The waiter interrupted with a request for dessert selections. I motioned across the table and glanced at the menu. I couldn't concentrate. My host ordered the cake.

"And for you, sir?"

"The tiramisu." An old standby.

I watched him collect the menus and walk off. My host resumed the conversation. "You're having a hard time believing that God would become a man."

"Well," I half chuckled, half snorted, "wouldn't you?"

"Maybe. It depends on what I expected from God."

"I don't expect him to look as if he just finished the day at Merrill Lynch."

He laughed gently. "No, I wouldn't either, I suppose."

I leaned back and folded my arms. "And to be honest, I really don't believe that God asks people just to take a blind leap of faith about him."

"You're right. He doesn't. That's what the world's religions do."

"What's the difference between them and what you're saying?"

"About one hundred eighty degrees. In this case God gives proof before he expects faith. But the world's religions have no evidence for their claims. Various forms of Hinduism count over three hundred million gods. What proof do they have of their existence?"

"None, as far as I'm concerned."

He motioned his index finger toward me. "That's why you're not a Hindu. You see no reason to believe it. What evidence can Buddhists offer that ultimate reality is an unknowable void called nirvana? Who can demonstrate to you that God actually spoke to Muhammad? Or to Joseph Smith of the Mormons? Or—"

"But Jesus is just the same. What evidence is there that Jesus was God?" I noticed that my elbows had migrated onto the table.

"Well, for one thing, that's exactly what God said would happen."

"When did he say that?"

He took a drink of water before continuing. "You've read some of the prophets."

"I never paid much attention to that Nostradamus stuff."

His brow furrowed. "The real ones," he insisted.

I had, in fact, read some of the Hebrew prophets. Elizabeth, my girlfriend back at NIU, had successfully goaded me into attending a dorm Bible study that covered them.

"They said the Messiah would come," I answered. "I don't think they ever said anything about his being God."

"You focused more on Elizabeth at that study than on the Bible. I suggest you reread Isaiah, Daniel, and Micah."

"How did you know—"

ASSYRIANS INVENTED ROMANS
CRUCIFIXIONS; PERFECTED IT

"I was there."

I looked intently at him for several moments. He kept his eyes on mine, but I couldn't read his expression. I ignored his last comment. "I know what they wrote. They said the Messiah would be born of a virgin, born in Bethlehem. They described his crucifixion, et cetera, et cetera."

"That's a pretty good tip-off, don't you think? Micah predicting seven centuries in advance the village where the Messiah would be born? David describing in detail death by crucifixion, centuries before the Romans invented the practice? Daniel telling the year of the Messiah's death, five hundred years ahead of time?"

"Really?" I was genuinely surprised. "What year?"

"Calculating by the Jewish calendar, AD 33."

I wasn't sure what to say to that. I emptied my wineglass.

He continued. "As for saying the Messiah would be God himself, the prophets said that he would be called Mighty God, Eternal Father, that he would be from days of eternity, that he would be worshiped."

That did sound eerily divine, but I wasn't about to admit it. "Still, that doesn't mean Jesus was God. Did you see that two-night miniseries they did on Jesus?"

"I know the one you're talking about."

"And that show Peter Jennings did awhile back on the historical Jesus?"

"Not particularly accurate."

"You say that, but how do we know? It portrayed Jesus as someone who never claimed to be the Messiah, much less God. It said he struggled with his identity, got swept up in events, and was killed as a political threat."

He answered matter-of-factly. "I forgave sins on my own authority, healed people, raised people from the dead, exercised power over nature, said I existed before Abraham, claimed to be one with the Father, said I was the giver of eternal life, and accepted worship. Who does that sound like to you?"

"Just because you claimed to be God doesn't mean that you are."

"No. But it does mean that I wasn't just a good religious teacher. Either I told the truth about who I am, or I lied, or I was insane. Those are the only real options. Good religious teachers don't claim to be God."

He looked off across the room, not seeming to focus on anything in particular. He shook his head almost imperceptibly, then looked back at me. "People distort the truth because they reject the final proof I've already given."

"What's that?"

"That I rose from the dead."

At that moment the waiter, easily within earshot of our

last exchange, appeared with our desserts. I avoided his eyes as he served them, refilled our water, and then departed. I spoke first.

"You're sitting here—alive—across the table from me. If you say you were once dead, it's pretty hard for me to prove otherwise."

He took a bite of a strawberry. "Good point. Why don't we deal with the actual facts? What do you know about me historically?"

His use of the first person still disconcerted me, but I could go for this topic. I plunged in. "From secular histories, we know Jesus was an actual person."

"Okay."

"We know he was a teacher who had a large following."

He nodded.

"We know the Romans executed him," I continued.

"Which brings us to the event in question. What happened then?"

"Well, his disciples claimed that he was raised from the dead, but of course they would claim that."

"Really? Is that what they expected to happen?"

I searched through my Sunday school data bank. "Not that I recall," I admitted.

"Despite the fact that I told them repeatedly it would."

"True."

"Did they believe it at first, when the women told them about it?"

"No."

"When did they believe?"

"According to their accounts, when they actually saw Jesus."

"So when these men wrote accounts of my life, they describe themselves as failing to believe beforehand, failing to believe afterward, and only believing after they were hit in the face with the evidence, and even then they stayed in hiding, afraid of the authorities. Is that the way you would portray yourself if you wanted people to follow you in a cause?"

"It's possible," I answered. *Improbable, perhaps, but possible.*

"For what purpose?" He lifted a fork to his cake. "So they could be impoverished, persecuted, and finally martyred?"

"Lots of people have died for believing something false."

"Yes, for a false philosophy or false religious belief. But this is different. We're talking about people who willingly died for their belief in a historical event. They were there. They saw whether it happened. They all said it happened, even though saying so brought them nothing but suffering and death. People don't die for something they know is a lie, especially when it brings them no benefit."

High-school debate had taught me a thing or two about argumentation. Like when to drop a losing point. I sampled my tiramisu and thought a moment. "Maybe they thought Jesus had died, when he really hadn't."

"How often do you think the Romans let people who had not yet died down off crosses?"

"Probably not too often."

"So you're implying the Romans let someone down so badly injured as to be left for dead, then two days later my recovery was so miraculous that the disciples thought I was God himself?"

"Okay, it's unlikely," I replied. "But the disciples did have something to gain from claiming Jesus had been resurrected."

"Go on."

"They had status to gain as those who began a new religious movement."

His answer surprised me. "You're right. They did have that status." He leaned forward and rested his fork on his dessert plate. "You're saying that the men who spread the word about me, who taught people to love one another, who told slave owners in a brutal society to treat their slaves well, who told husbands to love their wives at a time when women were treated as chattel, who told people to honor and obey the government that was martyring them, who launched the greatest force for good that the world has known, that they did all this based on something they knew to be false?"

"It hasn't all been good," I retorted. "What about the Crusades? Or the Salem witch trials? Or the Spanish Inquisition? What about Europe's Wars of Religion between the Protestants and the Catholics, or the fighting in Northern Ireland? Your own people are always at each other's throats."

His countenance changed noticeably, and he let out an audible sigh. "That's true." He remained silent for a few moments, looking at the table. "It makes me very sad."

The change in him disarmed me, taking me off the defensive and, frankly, off the offensive as well. I sat looking at him, then asked honestly, "Why has Christianity been such a mixed bag?"

He folded his hands on the table. "Several reasons. Most of the people who have done these things didn't really know me. They may have seemed outwardly religious, but they weren't mine. They never really put their trust in me."

"Pardon me for saying so, but that seems a little convenient for you."

"Not really. More than anything I wanted to have a relationship with them. But they wouldn't."

"Still," I countered, "you can't claim that no real Christians have perpetrated any of these things."

"No, I can't. That's the tragedy of it."

"It almost seems the norm."

He unfolded his hands and sat back. "It isn't. But it's been too frequent."

"Why?"

"Because they never learned to live as the new people they were."

"I'm not sure what you mean."

"When people put their trust in me and receive eternal life, they get more than forgiveness. Otherwise, heaven would be populated with a bunch of forgiven sinners still running from God. God won't have that."

"So what does he do about it?"

"He does more than forgive them. He changes them on the inside. Their heart, their human spirit, is actually made new. In the depths of their being they no longer run from God; they are joined to him. They no longer want to disobey God; they want to do what he says is good."

"But they don't do it," I objected.

"Often they do. But not always. A new heart gets you in the game. Then you have to let me be your instructor. I teach you how to live based on what's been made new on the inside. Some people don't let me do that. They'd rather do it their way. So they remain judgmental or selfish or fearful. There's no joy in that."

"This sounds almost New Agey, like something Dave and Paula would say."

"Maybe," he answered, "but it's not. Tell me, you've talked to your two friends enough. What do you think they're after?"

"Connection with the divine, I suppose. Except they believe they already are divine in a sense. It's a little confusing."

He nodded as he finished a bite of cake. "How do they try to connect with God?"

"More enlightenment," I replied, more as a question than as a statement. "Working on letting go of misguided desires and embracing"—my New Age vocabulary was failing me—"embracing something. I'm not sure what."

"They're trying to achieve through a lot of effort the very thing I offer for free."

"What's that?"

"When someone receives me, God forgives them, he makes them new on the inside, and"—he paused momentarily—"he comes to live in them."

I had been downing my tiramisu during his explanation, but this last statement caused me to halt an approaching bite. "He what?"

"He comes to live in them. That's as close to God as you can get. And unlike people trying to manufacture the connection on their own, it's the real thing."

I wasn't sure that sounded like a great deal. "The last thing I need is God looking over my shoulder every minute."

"He's already looking over your shoulder every minute. What you need is him living in you every minute."

"What for?"

"Well, for one, how else are you ever going to love your daughter unconditionally, to say nothing of Mattie? You want to love Mattie better, but you don't know how. And even if you did know, you don't have the ability. Only God loves that way. He wants to do it through you."

He was right. Despite my best intentions, things weren't going all that well with Mattie. I constantly found myself getting irritated with her, and she with me. I was afraid Nick the romancer had gone into hibernation. I picked up my fork, took a bite of tiramisu, and finally spoke. "I've never heard all this before."

"I know. My disciples knew it and lived it and passed it on. But the message got distorted along the way. Church hierarchies, power structures—they crowded it out. People wanted to reduce God to a set of rules. But he's not about rules, any more than marriage is about rules."

"Then what's he about?"

"Joining people to himself. He designed them to be joined to him, like man and woman are made to be united. People were meant to have God's very life in them. Without that, they're like a new SUV with no engine. They may look good, but they don't work. They're missing the most important part."

I leaned back to take in what he'd said. "If this is what Christianity is all about, why don't they say it?"

"Because most haven't understood. Some have, though. It's never been hidden. Read the last third of John's gospel. It's all there. Mr. McIntosh knew it."

"My seventh-grade science teacher. I always liked him."

"Believe it or not, he liked you too."

"All the times he sent me to detention?"

He smiled. "You didn't give him much choice, did you?"

"No." I smiled back. "I suppose I didn't."

I took another bite of my dessert, as did he. We sat silently for a couple of minutes as I cleaned my plate. I finally broke the silence.

"So. Where do we go from here?"

"That's a good question," he said. "Where do you want to go?"

I wasn't sure.

8

The Coffee

"WHY DOESN'T GOD just show himself to people?"

The waiter had walked off with our dessert plates. I had resisted the urge to scrape mine with my fork as I usually did at home. Waiting for coffee, I decided it was now or never to get some of my remaining questions about God and life answered. This one seemed like a decent place to start.

Jesus wiped his mouth with his napkin and returned it to his lap. "What would you have me do?"

"I don't know—appear to everyone personally."

He chuckled, and seeing the irony in my statement, I couldn't help but join him momentarily.

"No, seriously," I said. "Most people don't get a dinner invitation."

"I did appear to humanity. I became one of you. That's about as personal as it gets."

"But that was two thousand years ago."

"It doesn't matter. Most people didn't believe then, either. You don't have to see with your eyes to believe."

I rested an elbow on the back of my chair. "At least God could perform some kind of sign that would show he exists."

"I did that, too. They still didn't believe. My Father did that at Mount Sinai with the Jews. They turned away from him within six weeks."

The waiter appeared with our coffee orders: a cappuccino for me, regular coffee for him. He used a little cream, no sugar.

"It's not a matter of further visual evidence," he continued. "People have all the evidence they need. It's a matter of the heart. Do they want to trust God and humbly receive the gift he offers, or do they insist on proving themselves good enough and doing it their own way?"

Somehow his statements about "people" seemed to have a very personal application. I wanted to keep the conversation on a more impersonal level.

"But how can you say people have all the evidence they need?"

"They have creation to tell them that God exists. Humanity knows more than ever before how intricately designed and finely tuned creation is. People have me to tell them what God is like. That's one reason I came, to reveal the Father. They have my resurrection to prove I am God. They have the Bible as God's message to them."

I took my first sip of cappuccino, licking the foam off my lips as he drank some coffee. "My religion professor said so many copying errors were made over the years that we don't really know what the original Bible said."

He shook his head slightly as he put his cup down. "He doesn't do much research, does he? As I said before, he would find the opposite is true. It's been painstakingly copied. The number of places where you have a question of any consequence is minuscule."

I had to admit I hadn't done the research, either. I forged ahead. "But what about all the contradictions?"

"Like what?"

"I don't know. Like…I don't know specifics. I just know there are supposed to be contradictions."

He smiled. "I'll give you one. One gospel account says I healed two blind men outside of Jericho. Another says I healed one."

"There you go."

"Okay. The other day when you told Les that you and Mattie had gone to a movie, had the two of you gone alone?"

"No, Mattie's friend Jessica came with us."

"Why did you leave that fact out?"

"It wasn't relevant to the story I was telling."

"True."

I expected more, but he stopped there.

"Are you saying the Bible's historical accounts are true?"

"Your own archaeologists are telling you that. You should have renewed your subscription to *U.S. News & World Report.* Check out a cover story on it."

"But I can't believe that God really created the universe in six days or that the earth is only six thousand years old. That's preposterous."

"Who is asking you to believe that?"

"All those fundamentalists. They added up all the genealogies in Genesis and said that the earth was created six thousand years ago."

He took another sip of coffee. "Genesis presents a flow of history. It says that God created the universe in an orderly fashion, starting with light itself. He made the earth, then gave it design: forming continents out of the oceans, creating plant life, creating animal life, creating humanity in his image. Now, is there anything in that sequence that your scientists would disagree with?"

"Well, they wouldn't agree with the 'in God's image' part."

"No. That's their problem isn't it? They don't want to acknowledge that they are created in God's image, because that would make them accountable to a Creator. They don't want that."

"But what about all the miracles? Like Joshua marching

around Jericho seven days, then the walls falling. Or David plunking Goliath in the middle of the forehead. Or God parting the Red Sea."

"Are you implying that the Creator of the universe can't perform miracles?"

"You wouldn't even change my wine back into water." I was unable to restrain a slight smirk.

He returned to the miracles. "I'll grant you, David and Goliath would be hard to verify outside the Bible. But they've already discovered the ruins of Jericho. The city was built just as the Bible describes it. And the walls fell in exactly the manner described too."

"You're kidding."

"No. As for the Red Sea, give your archaeologists a couple of decades." He winked. "But that's not the real issue, is it?" He put down his coffee and leaned forward. "Remember how, when you were six, you couldn't believe a two-wheeled bike would stay upright under you, until you tried it and you saw that it would?"

"Sure."

"If you actually open up the Bible and ask God to speak to you, Nick, you'll see that he will."

We looked into one another's eyes a moment. I finally spoke again. "Not everyone has access to a Bible."

"No," he acknowledged, "not everyone does."

"So what does God do about them?"

"The Father asks people to respond to the revelation they've been given. That may only be creation and their conscience. That's what he holds them accountable for."

"But they never get to hear about you."

"If anyone is really willing to do what God asks, he will reveal himself to them."

I let out a disbelieving snort. "Well, if they don't have a Bible…"

"God can use whatever means he wishes. Usually he sends people. Sometimes in areas where the gospel is restricted, like in Muslim countries, I reveal myself in dreams."

"But it seems like people in some places have a huge advantage. They can hear about you all the time."

"Yes, and they ignore the message. As I said, God reveals himself to anyone willing to trust him. He provides his forgiveness to all who will accept it."

"And what about people who think they're good enough, like Mrs. Willard?"

"They will stand before God on their own merit." He lifted his cup to his lips once more, then returned it to the table. "That's not a position you want to be in. It's like a father who offers a billion-dollar inheritance to his son, but the son says to him, 'Not until I've proved myself worthy.' It seems noble to try to be good enough, but in reality it's just prideful obstinacy. The son wants the inheritance on his own terms. He doesn't want to accept it as a gift. But God offers it only as a gift. You can't earn it. No one can."

I took a long sip of my cappuccino, which had cooled some. This time I wiped off the foam with my napkin and placed it on the table instead of in my lap. I looked back up at him.

"Is there a hell?"

"Yes," he answered quietly. "For those who choose to stay separated from God, there is existence. It's not an existence you want."

I sat silently for a moment.

"What's it like?"

"If you remove all sources of good from life as you know it, that's what it's like. God is the source of all good. For those who choose separation from him, there is no good." He paused. "You can't even comprehend how bad that would be."

"Why does he send people there?"

"The Father offers forgiveness to anyone willing to receive him. People choose continued separation from God. He respects what they choose."

"But why doesn't he just make everyone go to heaven? They'd be happier there."

"Love doesn't force relationship," he said in a tone even softer than before. "If you had somehow forced Mattie to marry you, it wouldn't have been love. God created people to be able to choose freely. He honors their choices."

I thought about that for a moment. *Somehow it just doesn't seem ri—*

"You live in a world turned upside down by humanity's rebellion. Sometimes things don't make sense. When you don't let Sara play near the street, it doesn't make sense to her. One day it will. God loves with a love greater than you can know. He doesn't want anyone separated from him. But some will be. One day that will make sense."

"I don't find that answer entirely satisfying."

"I know," he replied. "That's okay."

I took another drink and gathered my thoughts. "I suppose you'll say that God allowing suffering is the same kind of thing."

"What do you think?"

"Based on what you've said, humanity suffers because it separated itself from God."

"Yes."

"So why doesn't he just make things right, right now? Why wait for some day in the future?"

He drank some coffee. "That's difficult to answer, because you can't see things from God's perspective right now. But there is a purpose to the present time. And one day everything will be made right."

"That doesn't quite seem fair, for God to work out his plan while we suffer."

"You're forgetting something. God didn't leave you to suffer alone. He suffered more than anyone."

I looked down at my cappuccino for a few moments. The foam had flattened out, and it was only lukewarm. I took a couple of sips, lost in my thoughts. Finally he spoke.

"You're angry about your dad."

"God took him away when I was sixteen. I'd say that's worth being mad about. Or was that just part of God's plan?" My voice was rising, and I glanced around to see if anyone had overheard me. *Oh, who cares?* I turned back to Jesus.

He sat silently, his eyes held on mine. "You loved your dad very much."

I glanced back at my cup and eventually spoke toward it. "We used to do a lot together—go fishing, go to Cub games, Blackhawk games. He had played some semipro hockey for a while, and he coached all my hockey teams. After Mother divorced him and we moved across town, he stopped coaching me… I probably could have played college."

"You still saw him, though."

I figured that was a statement, not a question. I answered anyway. "Yeah. Every other weekend. But it wasn't the same."

"He missed you too." That was definitely a statement.

I finally looked up. "I know."

"You don't know how brokenhearted he was about you. It almost killed him to lose you."

"Well, he didn't live much longer anyway, did he?" I didn't even bother trying to hide my anger this time.

"No." He spoke quietly. "He didn't."

I drank the last of my cappuccino.

"This won't seem true to you," he said, "but I was heartbroken for both of you."

I put my cup down and stared across the table, not feeling anger so much as lifelessness. "You're right; that doesn't seem true."

We sat in silence.

"So," I finally said, "you never answered my question. Was my parents' divorce and my dad's death part of God's plan?"

He took a moment to reply. "You know the story of the prodigal son."

"Yeah." *Great. Another Sunday school lesson.*

"What did it take for the son to return to the father, who loved him?"

I answered in a monotone, listless voice. "For life to get really bad, in the pigpen. So what?"

"Sometimes…it takes deep hurts for people to feel their need for God."

"And that's God's plan?"

"That's what God is willing to use in a broken world. Your dad's pain drove him to me. And without that wound in your heart, Nick, you wouldn't be sitting here talking with me, either."

I leaned back, folded my arms, and sighed. "I wish I could say it all makes sense now." I looked aside momentarily, then back at him. "I wish I could say that."

9

The Bill

THE RESTAURANT HAD emptied. I glanced around to where the table of six had laughed the evening away. It was reset for tomorrow's lunch. The young couple had long since left. Even a middle-aged pair in the corner who had entered during our entrée had departed. *Have we been talking that long?*

The place had the eerie quiet that comes when your party closes down a restaurant for the night. I could hear the *clink* of someone sorting utensils. Our waiter approached our table.

"Another cappuccino, sir?" he asked me.

"No, this was fine."

He looked toward Jesus. "And you, sir? More coffee?"

"No, thank you. We're ready for the bill."

"Yes, sir."

My eyes followed as he stepped toward the front of the restaurant. Turning back to the table, I saw Jesus loosening his tie for the first time.

"Even I don't like these things," he said.

God doesn't like neckties. Note that for future reference.

The waiter reappeared with a black leather bill holder and placed it on the table between us. He then turned to Jesus, held out a blank piece of paper and a pen, and in a hushed voice said, "Can I have your autograph, sir? Just in case."

Jesus smiled and took the pen and paper. "Of course." He wrote more than his name (I couldn't tell what) and handed it back to the waiter. *I wonder how much that'll go for on eBay.*

"Thank you very much, sir."

"Thank you, Eduardo," he replied.

Their eyes stayed on one another as they held the paper between them, then Eduardo took it, paused, and walked away.

For the first time since the meal began, I regarded my host. His features remained the same—the dark hair, the olive complexion, the almost black eyes, the toned muscles—but somehow his look had changed. He seemed at the same time softer and yet more authoritative. I wasn't entirely comfortable with him, yet I was strangely drawn to him.

Jesus turned back to me. "I like Eduardo. He's a humble man."

The longer we'd talked, the more questions had popped

into my mind. What was the universe like before the Big Bang? Is there intelligent life on other planets? What really happened to the dinosaurs? But with the bill on the table, one question overshadowed the others.

"You keep telling me that God offers me this free gift, eternal life. So what's heaven like?"

He smiled as if I had asked about his hometown. "Heaven is a cool place. Humanity's senses have been so dulled by living in this broken world, you wouldn't believe all the sights, sounds, smells. Colors you've never seen. Music you've never heard. Lots of activity, yet overwhelming peacefulness. Remember how you felt when you stood at the Grand Canyon—too awestruck to take it all in?"

"Yeah."

"Heaven is like that, only infinitely more."

"I feel stupid asking this, but are the streets really made of gold?"

He laughed. "Describing heaven isn't exactly easy. It's like explaining snow to a tribal native from the Amazon. He doesn't have a point of reference for it. What's written in the Bible is true, but in a way greater than you can imagine."

"And you're saying I don't have to do anything to get there?"

"You have to receive the gift of eternal life," he answered. "You can't trust in your own goodness. You have to put your faith in me." He shifted to the side and took a long drink of water, then put the glass down. "But you're confusing heaven and eternal life."

My mind was still partly on what heaven might look like, so I didn't quite take in his last statement. "What? I'm sorry."

"You're confusing heaven and eternal life."

"I thought they were the same thing."

"No."

"I'm not following you."

"Eternal life isn't a place," he responded. "And it's not primarily length of existence. I am eternal life. The Father is eternal life."

"I'm not sure I'm getting what you're saying."

"Just as God is the source of all physical life, he is also the source of all spiritual life. Think of it this way. God created your body to need food, air, and water. What happens when you remove those things?"

"You die."

"The same thing holds true for your spirit. God created your spirit to be joined with him. Without him, it's dead. It has no life. God is spirit, and he is life. The only way for you to have eternal life is to have him."

I still wasn't sure I was connecting all the dots. "So when you say God offers eternal life…"

"He is offering you himself. God comes to live within you forever. When you have me, you have Life itself. With a capital L."

I leaned back and thought that over for a moment. "So what is heaven?"

"Heaven is simply a place where I am."

"But people don't go to heaven until they die."

"True. But you can have eternal life right now."

I must have had a confused look on my face again.

"Eternal life isn't something that starts when you die," he continued. "It's something that starts the minute you receive me. When you put your trust in me, you are not only completely forgiven, but I also join myself to your spirit. I come to live within you."

"You? Sitting right there?"

"The Holy Spirit, if you wish. He and the Father and I are one."

"You know, I never really understood that whole Trinity thing. Father, Son, Holy Spirit..."

He smiled. "Join the crowd. You aren't meant to understand it."

"Are you saying I'm incapable of understanding it?"

"Yes."

I wasn't sure how to respond.

"God wouldn't be much of a God," he said, "if you could fully understand his nature. Humanity still hasn't figured out most of creation. The Creator is far greater than that."

The significance of what he'd been saying was slowly dawning on me. I didn't fully comprehend it, but I got the gist of it. I just wasn't sure about the implications. "I'm still not entirely comfortable with God coming to live in me. I like the forgiveness part. But this other—"

"Is the best part. You need someone to love you and accept you and want to be with you, even when you feel bad about yourself. Someone who will always be with you. Everyone needs that. God made you that way."

"Sara wants to be around me," I half joked.

"Wait till she's fifteen."

That seems ages away.

"And," he said, "to tell you the truth, you need someone to put some adventure back in your life. Remember the kid who used to go dirt biking on Highback Ridge?"

I felt a spark of energy at the mention of the place. "Several times I almost didn't make it off there."

"I know." A smile edged onto his face. "You were quite a daredevil."

He leaned forward, resting his forearms on the table. "You're bored, Nick. You were made for more than this. You're worried about God stealing your fun, but you've got it backward. You're like a kid who doesn't want to leave for Disney World because he's having fun making mud pies by the curb. He doesn't realize that what's being offered is so much better. There's no adventure like being joined to the Creator of the universe." He leaned back from the table. "And your first mission would be to let him guide you out of the mess you're in at work."

My expression froze, and my eyes locked on his. Two months earlier I had discovered that the company was fabricating data on its environmental testing results. I wasn't involved, but I knew enough to jeopardize my career if we were caught. *And he knows.*

"You want out," he said. "Why don't you leave?"

"But I can't quit. There aren't any jobs like mine in this area, and Mattie would kill me if we have to move again. She just got her graphics business back to where it was in Chicago."

"You know it cheats Mattie and Sara to have you working at Pruitt. Not only are you risking your career, it's draining you. You're not there for them."

I stared across the table at him. Just talking about this drained me. *He's right. But…*

"I just can't do that, not now."

"You need someone to give you strength to make that decision. Because it really will work out okay. I know it doesn't seem like it."

"That's the truth. Mattie would be furious. And then I'd be mad at her for reacting that way. And then…" *And then things would go downhill from there. For months.* This whole scenario was getting darker by the minute.

"What if someone lived in you who could love Mattie even when she's upset at you?"

That seems utterly impossible.

"It's not with God," he said.

"What?"

"Impossible. I can love her through you even when it's hardest for you. And in the day-to-day routine as well. She needs that."

I looked down to avoid his eyes. Talking about my work mess was bad enough; I certainly wasn't used to talking about this kind of stuff, especially with a guy. Even if he was Jesus. "I don't think God is exactly doing backflips over me."

He laughed, leaned back, and folded his hands behind his head. "You know one of the people I liked to hang around most when I was here before?"

I shook my head.

"I liked Nicodemus. He used to come and ask me questions. My answers always confounded him. But I liked seeing his eyes open to what we were talking about. He was a good man, but he held a seat on the ruling council, and they were dishonest with the people."

"Sounds like my kind of guy," I mumbled.

"You and he have more in common than just a name. In a good way, mostly."

He paused, glanced at the bill holder, then took a sip of water. As he did, I reached toward the bill. "Here, let me get this," I said. "I owe you one."

My hand grabbed the leather holder, but before I could move it, his hand landed on my wrist. I looked over at him.

"Nick, it's a gift."

I relaxed my grip on the leather and looked down toward his hand. Both his shirt and his suit jacket had slid slightly up his arm. My eyes locked on a large puncture scar on his wrist.

I stayed silent for a moment. "I thought they went through your hands."

He followed my eyes to the scar. "Most people think that. The stakes were nailed through the wrist to support the weight of my body. Hand tissue would tear apart if it had to hold the body up."

I let him have the check. He pulled two bills out of his front pocket, slid them inside the holder, and looked up at me.

"Are you ready?"

Home

WE WALKED TOWARD the front of the restaurant, past the lattice. *Funny, I almost bolted out this way awhile ago. Now I don't even want to leave.* I fell a pace or two behind, lost in my thoughts.

Did I really just have dinner with… Why me?… Does he do this all the time?… What am I going to tell Mattie?… When I wake up tomorrow… What do I do now?

I looked up and watched as Jesus conversed briefly with Carlo, who'd been sweeping the foyer. They hugged before Carlo opened the door for him. I followed. We paused under the awning.

"You and Carlo act like old friends."

"We are."

"How long have you been coming to Milano's?"

"This is my first time."

He took a step toward my car. We walked in silence across the parking lot. I should have guessed he would know which car was mine, but I wasn't yet accustomed to being with someone who knew everything. We stopped at the Explorer.

"Which car is yours?" I was curious to know which one God preferred.

"Oh, I didn't drive."

I let that one hang.

It felt a little uncomfortable at my car. How do you say good-bye to Jesus? He didn't seem uneasy, though.

"Thanks for dinner," I finally said. Suddenly an earlier question popped back into my mind. "You never told me who sent the invitation."

He chuckled a little but didn't respond.

"I suppose this was your idea from the start."

"Actually, it was yours, Nick. Do you remember when your dad left, and you asked God to come and tell you why?"

"Not really."

"Well, I remembered. I've been planning this dinner for a long time."

I wasn't sure what to say. I fumbled in my pocket for my keys, pulled them out, and unlocked the car. I wanted to tell him how glad I was that I had stayed and how the evening had turned out so differently than I had expected. He knew, I suppose, but I wanted to say it anyway. All that came out, though, was, "Will we get together for dinner again?"

He smiled gently. "That's up to you."

"I'm not sure what that means."

"Yes, you are. Hand me your other business card."

I pulled out my billfold and gave him my last one. He pulled his pen out of his coat pocket, wrote something on the back of the card, then slid it inside my shirt pocket.

"That'll tell you how to reach me."

He grasped the door handle and opened it. "Mattie is already asleep. You'd better get home."

I still had a thousand questions. But he was right. I climbed in the car, turned the key, and rolled my window down. Probably sensing my uncertainty, he initiated the farewell. "I'm glad you showed up, Nick. I've enjoyed our time."

"I have too."

"Remember: I'm for you. Mattie is too. She just hasn't learned to show it very well yet. Give her time. Love her."

"I will."

"Kiss Sara for me."

"I will."

I reached out my right hand to him. He took it and shook it firmly. I couldn't help glancing at the scar on his wrist once more. Reluctantly I pulled my hand back and put the Explorer in reverse.

"Good-bye," I said.

"Until next time," he replied.

I backed out, then started across the parking lot. Looking through the rearview mirror, I waved. But he was gone.

The drive home from Milano's takes about twenty minutes. It seemed to take two. My mind traveled a thousand times faster than the wheels did. I pulled into the driveway, cutting my lights early so as not to wake anyone. I killed the engine and, as I reached for my coat, remembered my business card that Jesus had written on. I slid it out of my pocket and turned it over. "Revelation 3:20" was all it said. *Revelation 3:20. A Bible verse? The book of Revelation?* I got out of the car and quietly shut the door.

The house was silent as I locked everything up. Mattie had left a single lamp on for me in the living room. Gretel raised her head as I passed by the kitchen. I stopped and gave her a pat. "Sorry you didn't get your walk tonight, girl," I whispered. She put her head back down, resuming her sleep. *I hope Mattie remembered to feed her.*

I tiptoed up the stairs and peeked into Sara's room. Sound asleep. I crept to the crib and gave her a good-night kiss. Her breathing altered slightly, then returned to its normal rhythm.

I turned around and walked down the hall to our bedroom. *I'm not sure what I'm getting myself into here.* Reaching across the bed, I closed a novel Mattie had fallen asleep reading.

"Hi," I whispered. "I'm home."

Mattie roused slightly, groaned a little, then cracked her eyes. "Hello, honey," she mumbled.

"I'm really sorry about tonight, Mattie—"

"I know. It's okay. Let's talk about it in the morning."

"Okay."

I kissed her and pulled the covers up to her head.

"I'll be here shortly."

"Okay," she said in a slight daze as she rolled over to sleep.

I went to the study, where I could undress without disturbing her. I found a hanger for my suit pants in the closet. Then I decided to look for something else. I crossed the room, closed the door, and returned to the closet, quietly pulling out boxes of books that we didn't have space to put on our bookshelves. I emptied three boxes, but no luck. *It's got to be here somewhere.* Piles of books littered the floor as I started my fourth box. *I am making a total mess.* Then, pay dirt. My old Bible. I hadn't opened it since college. *I'm surprised I even kept this thing.* I turned to the back where Revelation was, then glanced again at my business card. "3:20."

I turned to chapter 3. Verse 20 was on the next page. It was a quote from Jesus:

> Here I am! I stand at the door and knock;
> if anyone hears my voice and opens the door,
> I will come in to him and will dine with him,
> and he with me.

Readers Guides

Here are three group readers guides to help you delve further into the content and meaning of *Dinner with a Perfect Stranger*.

The first guide is for a single evening event and features questions that are geared toward those without much background in Christian faith, Jesus, God, and the church. One fun thing to do is to create an actual dinner party event and have a group discussion of *Dinner with a Perfect Stranger*.

The second guide is designed for a four-week overview of the book. Ideal for reading groups and small groups, with this guide you can cover the content of *Dinner with a Perfect Stranger* in just one month.

The third guide is intended for a more intensive study of the book. Covering eight weeks, this study becomes a great tool for longer discussion and more in-depth explorations of faith and relationship with Jesus Christ.

ONE-EVENING READERS GUIDE

1. What was your initial reaction to the premise of the book? If you received an invitation like Nick received, what would be your reaction and response?

2. Do you ever wish you could have some sit-down-and-talk time with God? Why? If you could sit down one-on-one with Jesus, what are two questions you would like to ask him?

3. From the characterization in the book, how would you describe Jesus? What kind of person is he? What qualities of his stand out to you the most?

4. Is there such a thing as actual reality? Why is it important for our belief system to correspond to reality? What difference does it make if it does not? What's wrong with saying about someone's belief system that "It's true for them"?

5. How is belief in God not a blind leap of faith? How is belief in Jesus as God in the flesh not a blind leap of faith?

6. How do the gospel accounts make it clear that Jesus was not simply a good religious teacher?

7. What is unique about Jesus compared to the founders of other world religions?

8. On page 28, Jesus makes the statement, "You don't want what you're ultimately trusting to be wrong." What are you ultimately trusting concerning your eternal destiny?

9. Why in the book does Jesus say there is no path to God? What is the distinction he draws between "path" and "way"? What is the way?

10. Why isn't God interested in having people try to perform for him? What is the implication of this for your own

life? Why do people so easily believe that their efforts at being good will gain acceptance for them with God?

11. Where would you place yourself on the Mother Teresa-to-Hitler scale? Where does that put you in relation to God's perfect standard? Why?

12. How would you answer the question that Jesus poses on page 53: "On what basis are you going to stand before a perfectly holy God and say that you've been good enough?"

13. Which of the following aspects of the good news of Jesus Christ appeals to you the most:
    - getting your sins forgiven
    - being with God in eternity
    - having a real relationship with God now
    - receiving a changed heart with new desires from God
    - God living in you now and forever

14. What is the personal application for you of Revelation 3:20, the Bible verse that the book closes with?

15. If you have not received the free gift of eternal life from God that Jesus explains on page 58, what is keeping you from doing so now?

FOUR-WEEK READERS GUIDE

Week One: Chapters 1–4

1. What was your initial reaction to the premise of the book?

2. Do you ever wish you could have some sit-down-and-talk time with God? Why? If you could sit down one-on-one with Jesus, what are two questions you would like to ask him?

3. Is there such a thing as actual reality? Why is it important for our belief system to correspond to reality? What difference does it make if it does not?

4. What's wrong with saying about someone's belief system that "It's true for them"?

5. How is Christianity distinct from the other primary world views, such as Islam, Hinduism, and atheistic naturalism (the material world is all there is)?

6. How does the Christian concept of God differ from the Islamic concept of God? Why does this matter in regard to humanity's deepest longings? How does your experience relate to this?

7. On page 28, Jesus makes the statement, "You don't want what you're ultimately trusting to be wrong." What are you ultimately trusting concerning your eternal destiny? How do you know whether you will be with God for all eternity?

8. What are you trusting in the day-to-day aspects of your life, to live life to the fullest?

Week Two: Chapters 5–6

1. Why isn't God interested in having people try to perform for him? What is the implication of this for your own life?

2. If God's business is restoring relationships, what does he want your response to be toward him? toward others?

3. What do you think are the primary indicators that humanity is in rebellion against God?

4. Are there rips in the fabric of your life that only God is big enough to fix? Do you go to him with these things? How do you think he wants to use those rips for good in your life (Romans 8:28–29)? How can you cooperate with God in his fixing process?

5. How does Islam water down God's perfect holiness and justice? What is the way God can be both perfectly just and forgiving at the same time (see Romans 3:23–26)?

6. How would you answer the question Jesus poses to Nick on page 56: "Don't you think God loves you at least as much as you love Sara?"

7. Discuss the parable Jesus tells of the two schoolboys. How would you describe the character of the friend with the better grades? How is God like this friend, only more so? Why?

8. What should be the impact on your life of knowing that God longs to have you with him, both in eternity and in your daily life now?

9. If you have not received the free gift from God that Jesus explains on page 58, what is keeping you from doing so now?

Week Three: Chapters 7–8

1. How is belief in God not a blind leap of faith? How is belief in Jesus as God in the flesh not a blind leap of faith?

2. What happens to people on the inside when they place their trust in Jesus Christ?

3. If Jesus came to restore us to our original design, is God living in us part of how we were designed to live? What are the implications of this for your own life?

4. What aspects of your life would you like to change, but you don't seem to have the strength to do so? How does God want to be the one to do them through you?

5. In what sense is marriage "not about rules"? Why can God's relationship with us be described the same way?

6. What does it mean to you personally that God became human?

7. Jesus said that he came to reveal the Father. Based on what you know about Jesus, how would you describe God the Father?

8. Most of the New Testament teaching on hell comes from Jesus himself. How does knowing this affect your view of hell?

9. How would you explain God's purpose for the present time? In what sense will one day everything be made right?

10. What are the implications of the fact that God chose to suffer more than his creation suffered?

11. Are there hurts in your life that it seems God doesn't care

about? If you are willing to share, what is one of them? What does this chapter have to say about whether God actually cares or not?

12. How does God use personal pain in his plan of restoring his relationship with people? Have there been wounds in your heart that have driven you to God? What were/are they? How did they drive you to him?

Week Four: Chapters 9–10

1. Are you stuck on a performance basis with God, trying to please him through your own efforts? How does he want you to depend on him living through you instead?

2. In what way is "God living in you" the best part of the message of Jesus? What difference should it make if God lives in us?

3. If God lives in you, is it possible to love those whom you don't have a positive emotional response to, at least at times? How does this happen in a practical sense?

4. Read the gospel of Luke, chapter 15. If you have placed your trust in Jesus as your Savior, is God "doing backflips" over you? What is the implication of that for you?

5. From the characterization in the book, how would you describe Jesus? What kind of person is he? What qualities of his stand out to you the most?

6. Which of the following aspects of the good news of Jesus Christ is most important to you:

- getting your sins forgiven
- being with God in eternity
- having a real relationship with God now
- receiving a changed heart with new desires from God
- God living in you now and forever

7. Overall, what was the most important aspect of the book to you personally?

8. What questions remain in your mind concerning any of the issues the book raised? Is getting an answer to these questions important to you? How are you going to go about getting your answers?

9. What is the personal application for you of Revelation 3:20, the Bible verse that the book closes with? How can we dine with Jesus daily?

10. What action step(s) would you like to take concerning yourself as a result of reading this book?

11. What action step(s) would you like to take concerning someone else as a result of reading this book?

EIGHT-WEEK GROUP READERS GUIDE

Week One: Chapters 1–3

1. What was your initial reaction to the premise of the book? Does this say anything about where you are at this time in your life?

2. What about Nick's character can you relate to?

3. Do you ever wish you could have some sit-down-and-talk time with God? Why?

4. If you received an invitation like Nick received, what would be your reaction and response?

5. If you could sit down one-on-one with Jesus, what are two questions you would like to ask him?

6. Why do you think Jesus refused to turn the wine into water at the end of chapter 2? What does this say about having a faith relationship with God?

7. What is your reaction to Nick's statement ending chapter 3? Why?

Week Two: Chapter 4

1. Is there such a thing as actual reality? Why is it important for our belief system to correspond to reality? What difference does it make if it does not?

2. What's wrong with saying about someone's belief system that "It's true for them"?

3. How is Christianity distinct from the other primary world views, such as Islam, Hinduism, and atheistic naturalism (the material world is all there is)?

4. What would you say is the most convincing evidence that there is a Creator? Why?

5. How does the Christian concept of God differ from the

Islamic concept of God? Why does this matter in regard to humanity's deepest longings? How does your experience relate to this?

6. What is unique about Jesus compared to the founders of other world religions?

7. On page 28, Jesus makes the statement, "You don't want what you're ultimately trusting to be wrong." What are you ultimately trusting concerning your eternal destiny?

8. What are you trusting in the day-to-day aspects of your life, to live life to the fullest?

Week Three: Chapter 5

1. What aspect of the good news of Jesus Christ is emphasized in this chapter?

2. Why in the book does Jesus say there is no path to God? What is the distinction he draws between "path" and "way"? What is the way?

3. Why isn't God interested in having people try to perform for him? What is the implication of this for your own life?

4. Why do people so easily believe that their efforts at being good will gain acceptance for them with God?

5. How can there be benefit in obeying God if it won't get you into heaven?

6. If God's business is restoring relationships, what does he want your response to be toward him? toward others?

7. What do you think are the primary indicators that humanity is in rebellion against God?

8. Are there rips in the fabric of your life that only God is big enough to fix? Do you go to him with these things? How do you think he wants to use those rips for good purpose in your life (Romans 8:28–29)? How can you cooperate with God in his fixing process?

Week Four: Chapter 6

1. Why is it important that God be perfectly holy and perfectly just?

2. Where would you place yourself on the Mother Teresa-to-Hitler scale? Where does that put you in relation to God's perfect standard? Why?

3. To what degree have you participated in the "daily sins of the heart" that is the cancer of God's universe?

4. How would you answer the question that Jesus poses on page 53: "On what basis are you going to stand before a perfectly holy God and say that you've been good enough?"

5. How does Islam water down God's perfect holiness and justice?

6. How can God be both perfectly just and forgiving at the same time (see Romans 3:23–26)?

7. How would you answer the question Jesus poses to Nick on page 56: "Don't you think God loves you at least as much as you love Sara?"

8. Discuss the parable Jesus tells of the two schoolboys (pages 56 and 57). How would you describe the character of the friend with the better grades? How is God like this friend, only more so? Why?

9. What should be the impact on your life of knowing that God longs to have you with him, both in eternity and in your daily life now?

10. If you have not received the free gift from God that Jesus explains on page 58, what is keeping you from doing so now?

Week Five: Chapter 7

1. How is belief in God not a blind leap of faith? How is belief in Jesus as God in the flesh not a blind leap of faith?

2. Did any of the prophecies concerning the coming Messiah on page 63 surprise you? Which ones? Which of the prophecies is most important to you personally? Why?

3. How do the gospel accounts make it clear that Jesus was not simply a good religious teacher?

4. In what way does all of Christianity rest upon Jesus's rising from the dead? What good news did Jesus have to offer if he did not rise from the dead?

5. In what ways does the disciples' behavior in the weeks, months, and years after Jesus's crucifixion support the claim that Jesus rose from the dead? If Jesus did not rise

from the dead, how would you account for the disciples' lives and teaching as indicated on pages 66 and 67?

6. What happens to people on the inside when they place their trust in Jesus Christ?

7. In what sense is New Age religion a counterfeit of what God truly offers? Why do people find the counterfeit appealing?

8. If Jesus came to restore us to our original design, is God living in us part of how we were designed to live? What are the implications of this for your own life?

9. What aspects of your life would you like to change, but you don't seem to have the strength to do so? How does God want to be the one to do them through you?

10. In what sense is marriage "not about rules"? Why can God's relationship with us be described the same way?

Week Six: Chapter 8

1. What does it mean to you personally that God became human?

2. Why is trusting God a matter of the heart, not a matter of what the eyes do or do not see? Explain.

3. Why does God offer eternal life only as a gift instead of something you can earn?

4. Jesus said that he came to reveal the Father. Based on what you know about Jesus, how would you describe God the Father?

5. Why does Jesus say to Nick on page 77, "But that's not the real issue, is it?" What is the real issue in you placing your faith in Christ, either for your eternal destiny or your daily life?

6. Most of the New Testament teaching on hell comes from Jesus himself. How does knowing this affect your view of hell?

7. Why do you think anyone would choose continued separation from God?

8. How would you explain God's purpose for the present time? In what sense will one day everything be made right?

9. What are the implications of the fact that God chose to suffer more than his creation suffered?

10. Are there hurts in your life that it seems God doesn't care about? If you are willing to share, what is one of them? What does this chapter have to say about whether God actually cares or not?

11. How does God use personal pain in his plan of restoring his relationship with people? Have there been wounds in your heart that have driven you to God? What were/are they? How did they drive you to him?

Week Seven: Chapter 9

1. Are you stuck on a performance basis with God, trying to please him through your own efforts? How does he want you to depend on him living through you instead?

2. Explain how eternal life and heaven are not the same thing. Based on what Jesus says, how would you describe eternal life?

3. What aspects of God seem mysterious to you? Can other members of the group shed some light on these mysteries? Will some aspects of God always be a mystery to us?

4. In what way is "God living in you" the best part of the message of Jesus? What difference should it make if God lives in us?

5. Have you lost the spark or adventure in life? How should being joined to the Creator of the universe change that?

6. In what sense is your life still like the child making mud pies by the curb? What would it take for you to choose to go to Disney World instead?

7. Would God design life with him in eternity to be boring or to be the fulfilling enjoyment of all you were designed to be? What makes you say so? What are the implications of your answer for you?

8. If God lives in you, is it possible to love those whom you don't have a positive emotional response to, at least at times? How does this happen in a practical sense?

9. Read the gospel of Luke, chapter 15. If you have placed your trust in Jesus as your Savior, is God "doing back-flips" over you? What is the implication of that for you?

Week Eight: Chapter 10

1. What would you expect to happen in Nick's life now?

2. From the characterization in the book, how would you describe Jesus? What kind of person is he? What qualities of his stand out to you the most?

3. Which of the following aspects of the good news of Jesus Christ is most important to you:
   - getting your sins forgiven
   - being with God in eternity
   - having a real relationship with God now
   - receiving a changed heart with new desires from God
   - God living in you now and forever

4. What is the personal application for you of Revelation 3:20, the Bible verse that the book closes with?

5. How can we dine with Jesus daily?

6. What was the most important aspect of the book to you personally?

7. What questions remain in your mind concerning any of the issues the book raised? Is getting an answer to these questions important to you? How are you going to go about getting your answers?

8. What action step(s) would you like to take concerning yourself as a result of reading this book?

9. What action step(s) would you like to take concerning someone else as a result of reading this book?

About the Author

DAVID GREGORY is the best-selling author of *A Day with a Perfect Stranger, The Next Level, The Last Christian,* and the coauthor of the nonfiction book, *The Rest of the Gospel.* After a ten-year business career, he returned to school to study religion, sociology, and communications. He holds master's degrees from Dallas Theological Seminary and the University of North Texas. A native of Texas, he now lives in the Pacific Northwest.

You're Invited

www.DinnerWithAPerfectStranger.com

• Read the reviews

• Tell us what you think

• Download a readers guide

• Meet the author